Sherlock Holmes
and
The Adventure
of
The Iron Crown

Raymond Louis James Lovato
&
Michael Black

Airship 27 Productions

™

"Sherlock Holmes and the Adventure of the Iron Crown"
©2022 Raymond Louis James Lovato & Michael A. Black

Cover illustration ©2022 Morgan Fitzsimons
Interior illustrations © 2022 Rob Davis

Editor: Ron Fortier
Associate Editor: Gordon Dymowski
Production Designer: Rob Davis
Marketing Manager: Michael Vance

Published by
Airship 27 Productions
www.airship27.com
www.airship27hangar.com

ISBN: 978-1-953589-18-7

Printed in the United States of America

10 9 8 7 6 5 4 3 2 1

Dedication:

From Ray:
This is dedicated to the love of my life.
My light in the darkness.
The hand that holds mine tight
When my world comes crashing down.
Whose eyes I see upon waking each morning,
Whose lips I kiss every night.
To my sweet Angel,
Susan

Dedication:

From Mike:
For Ron Fortier, who gave us the chance to do this one. Stay strong, brother. Army strong. And also for Rob Davis whose artistic brilliance brought the scenes to life.

Sherlock Holmes
and
The Adventure
of
The Iron Crown

Raymond Louis James Lovato
&
Michael A. Black

PROLOGUE

Of the many cases in which my friend and associate, Sherlock Holmes, and I had been involved through our long association, one stood out in my memory as being particularly mysterious and vexing almost above all others. It was, as Holmes so aptly put it, a riddle wrapped in an enigma inside of a mystery. I am certain that particular description will someday be stolen, but, as you shall soon see, its relevance is startlingly apropos. However, although this one case in particular will forever stand out in my mind, I found myself reluctant to provide the accompanying chronicle. Both Holmes and I agreed that this was one case in which we should be sworn to secrecy due to the principals involved, to wit: a secret that was centuries old that concerned the most holy of relics, kept by covert societies and clandestine brotherhoods that exist on the edges of the known and unknown. We were able to make our way through the convolutions of those secret societies which operate in the light of day, but stretch their dark tentacles under the surface in the fashion of a gigantic squid. Thus, I have recounted it to the best of my ability, and vowed to let it remain in the tin dispatch box with the rest of my manuscripts, never to see the light of day during our lifetimes. However, the significance of this adventure was so compelling that I felt it would be an injustice to the memory and achievements of the world's greatest consulting detective should it not be memorialized in some fashion. So I now undertake to complete this telling, even if my own eyes might be the only ones to read it.

I respectfully now submit, *The Adventure of the Iron Crown*.

CHAPTER 1
THE FIRE

It was early on a dreary Tuesday morning as I stood there looking out the window of our lodging at 221 B Baker Street, where a cheerless drizzle formed haloes around the still-lighted gas lamps that cast a flickering light over the slow moving brougham as it drew to a halt in front of our quarters. A flash of lightning briefly made the scene resemble a sketchy black and white tableau, like a grainy photograph. The wind picked up slightly causing the cab's occupant to tightly clutch at his derby as he paid the driver and hurried toward our front door.

I had no doubt that he'd come to see my fellow lodger, Mr. Sherlock Holmes. After all, what else could draw someone out on such a dreadful morning?

I moved closer to the window pane and stared down at him to confirm my suspicion. He stood there in the wind for several moments as if as if he was waiting for it and the rain to subside. Finally, he dashed to the front door, raised his hand and rang the doorbell. It went without saying that Mrs. Hudson would usher him in and then come up to advise us of the caller.

Wanting to demonstrate my powers of deduction to Holmes, I turned and said, "I believe we're about due for a visitor."

Holmes, who was seated in his customary stuffed chair next to the desk containing his elaborate concoction of glass tubes, beakers, and his assortment of chemicals, removed his long-stemmed pipe from his mouth and said, "Quite right, old boy. I wonder why he took so long to ring the bell in this inclement weather?"

I was stunned. How could Holmes have possibly known of the man's hesitation? He certainly was nowhere near the window, as I had been. I knew I had mere moments to ask him before Mrs. Hudson's arrival and announcement, so I did.

"Come now, Holmes. How the devil did you know about the man's hesitation?"

The detective replaced the pipe in his mouth, drew upon it, and then released a plume of grayish smoke. He was smoking that dreadful Turkish tobacco again and the odor it gave off was pungent.

"I saw you standing by the window," he said. "You were initially focused on the weather, no doubt, and then something else piqued your interest. The sounds of the hansom cab's arrival were audible to me even this far from the window. Peripherally, I then observed you move fractionally closer to the glass, and surmised that you were watching something or someone below. The sound of the cab's arrival did little to alter your intense stare, so it had to be the passenger who was discharged. The time that elapsed between that arrival and the subsequent ringing of the doorbell was such that the person below was unsure he wanted to step out in this miserable storm. Then after the space of several seconds, he relented and rang the bell."

"Amazing," I muttered, always fascinated by my friend's extraordinary powers of deduction.

I heard the pitter-patter of Mrs. Hudson's feet as she traversed the seventeen steps to our door and knocked. Holmes folded the top half of the *Daily Telegraph* into his lap and in his usual monotone said, "Come in, Mrs. Hudson."

The door swung open and our landlady entered with her salver bearing a slightly damp calling card. "An Inspector Stanley Hopkins to see you, Mr. Holmes."

"Ah," he said. "Hopkins, one of Scotland Yard's finest, which isn't the kindest of accolades. I wonder what brings him out on such a dreary morning? Please show him up."

"I will," she said, raising a reproachful eyebrow in his direction. "But please, don't you let him go dripping all over the carpet."

"Of course, your carpet is as safe as the crown jewels, Mrs. Hudson." There was a smile on his thin lips as he leapt up brandishing the folded newspaper. "I shall instruct the inspector to remain on the confines of this newspaper until he has dripped to dryness."

Mrs. Hudson beamed at him, turned, and left.

Holmes spread the newspaper out on the carpet and stepped back. He was wearing his purple dressing gown over some brown pants.

Mrs. Hudson returned and stood in the doorway, motioning for the inspector to come join her on the landing. From the sound of it, he bounded up the stairs like an eager puppy having just been called by his master. Doffing his hat to Mrs. Hudson he entered our study. He was a tall, lean man with a well-trimmed moustache and a firm jaw and, according to Holmes, held a good grasp of the law.

Before he could utter a word, Holmes held up his hand and then pointed to the spread of newspaper on the floor.

"If you would be so kind, Inspector," Holmes said. "As to remain on that rampart until such time as the rain drops have divested themselves from your overcoat."

Hopkins gave a start, and then stepped onto the paper.

"Most certainly," he said, but from his tone, his irritation was evident.

I was most happy to see Hopkins because in the past, whenever he came calling on Holmes and myself, he always brought the most interesting cases, ones that piqued the detective's curiosity. His timing couldn't have been more perfect for in the past two weeks the only case that my companion had worked on was that of a woman with a spurious claim to nobility who was engaged to a rich import merchant from the upper West End. It was hardly worth the enormous talents of my brilliant friend, and I was afraid that the ennui, that black cloud of boredom that fell over him from time to time when his great mind wasn't occupied with a truly fascinating conundrum, would cause him to slip back into the usage of his dreaded seven percent solution. I didn't want to see that happen once again to my friend. As it stood, he hadn't touched the needle in several weeks.

"Good morning, Mr. Holmes. Dr. Watson," Hopkins said. "Thank you for seeing me."

"Well, we could hardly let you stand out there in the rain, now could we?" Holmes said.

"'Tis a truly a dismal morning out there. The sewers are already backed up by Old Marylebone Town Hall."

"Really?" I interjected.

"Well," Holmes said. "I do hope that you haven't come here just to deliver a weather report." He strode forward walking in a circle around the inspector. "The gutters will be, as Jonathan Swift once said, awash with man and beast as well as the detritus of humanity."

"I don't recall him saying that," I said.

"If he did not," Holmes said, pausing to give Hopkins's overcoat a shake, sending the last remnants of accumulated raindrops onto the newspaper spread. "Then he should have." He withdrew the long-stemmed pipe from his mouth once again and raised an eyebrow. "Please shake off the remainder of that rain and then have a seat."

My friend stepped back as Hopkins brushed the residual moisture from his garment.

"That should do it, eh?" he said.

"Quite," Holmes said, motioning to the chair directly across from him and next to the fire. Hopkins obligingly took the seat offered to him by my companion.

On the several occasions that he worked with us Hopkins showed himself to be a student of Holmes and the ways of deductive reasoning and investigation; but ultimately proved, like most at Scotland Yard, not very good at it. He had trouble, once latching onto a conclusion, of not considering an alternative solution as the facts might present themselves. But he wasn't afraid to ask for help, having come to us before to seek our aid. Holmes had once referred to him as a promising detective with a congenial personality.

"Well," Hopkins began. "I assume that you have read about the fire at the Free Mason Temple last evening?"

"The Free Masons," I said. "What the devil are they up to now?"

Holmes ignored my question. "As a matter of fact, I did see a limited account of it in the morning paper." He gestured toward the pages on the floor and smiled slightly. "In fact, I believe you were standing on it."

Hopkins's eyebrows rose. "I was?"

"Let's not stand on ceremony," Holmes said. "As I recall, the fire took place around ten o'clock last evening, which gave little time for much detail in the morning papers."

"I've come to you about that, Mr. Holmes."

"I'm afraid I have little interest in fires," he said, pressing the tips of his fingers together to form a steeple. "I concentrate on unusual murders or extraordinary burglaries. Unless this fire was started by Satan himself, along with a hellish burglary, I doubt it would hold much interest for me."

My hopes that Holmes would be somehow engaged were dashed as I saw him glance toward the mantel where the syringe and the vial with the snowy white serpent resided.

"You mean a burglary like the South End Market Snatches?" Hopkins asked. "I'll have you know that I was the lead detective on that case. I'm rather proud of my work on that one, I am. It took over two months of diligent investigating to solve that one."

"Quite," said Holmes, "I remember Dr. Watson reading me the newspaper accounts of it several months ago. The incident actually held little interest for me, but every other day it seemed that a new article was printed with a new fact or two about the case. It seemed to catch Watson's attention" A smile graced his lips as he glanced at me.

"So to ease my mind," I said, "after the fourth day's report, he told me that it was the delivery service acting in collusion with the dock foreman who was responsible."

Hopkins's jaw dropped open.

"Quite an elementary deduction," Holmes added. "A simple one, actually."

"But it took me two months," Hopkins said, his face bearing traces of humiliation and bewilderment. "How did you figure it out so fast?"

Holmes allowed the pipe stem to rest of his lower lip as he said, "Eliminate the impossible, and whatever remains, no matter how improbable, is the answer."

The only sound in the room was the crackling of the fire. Hopkins sat there, motionless, somewhere between stunned and embarrassed. I actually felt a bit sorry for him.

"Do go on," my companion urged. "The fire?"

"Yes, the fire," Hopkins said. "A little after ten last evening, I arrived at the Free Mason Temple on Whitmore Way North West and the Stockwood Exchange. The building was still smoldering. The fire brigade had the situation pretty much under control, what with the rain helping them. It was around eleven that Fire Battalion Chief Polk told me it was clear to enter the office and library where the fire was contained to survey the scene. But I must tell you, Mr. Holmes, I had to argue for many minutes with a Mason called Mr. Pounder who was not going to allow me into the building to inspect the scene. Something about the solemn secrecy of the Masonic rights and some such nonsense."

"Typical of those buggers," I said. "Always hiding their activities behind secret emblems and ritualistic handshakes."

Hopkins nodded at my affirmation and continued.

"Anyway, I told him that if he insisted on interfering with an official investigation by Scotland Yard I would see him hauled down to the Yard and detained there until I finished up. He relented." His chest seemed to swell with pride at his reminiscence. "That's when I entered and Chief Polk showed me the body of the Master Mason Dr. Robert Withermew, dead, in his office. And it wasn't from the fire. The front of his head was bashed in from a cudgel."

"Was he a medical doctor?" I asked.

Hopkins shook his head. "No. It was an honorary title bestowed upon him for his scholarly pursuits."

"A bunch of poppycock, if you ask me," I said.

Holmes seemed to perk up at this latest admission. "What else can you tell me about this Withermew?"

"Well, he's about seventy years old, slightly overweight for his size, receding white hair. Wore pince-nez glasses."

The detective's expression foretold of his impatience. "Yes, and apparently had a large indentation in his head from being struck. Did he have any enemies?"

I had to smile at Holmes's apparent agitation.

"No, sir. Everyone I interviewed described him as friendly, a gentle soul. Not a person in the world held any ill will against him."

"Well, someone obviously did," the detective snorted. "Where was the body found?"

"Lying between the office and the library, Mr. Holmes."

Holmes removed the pipe from his mouth, set it aside on the small table, and leaned back in the chair with his eyes closed. "Tell me about this office and adjoining library?"

"There's a large antechamber with one corner dedicated to Dr. Withermew's desk and effects. The office must be approximately two hundred square feet. The library next door is quite impressive as well. Over forty square yards if it's a foot."

"And who first saw the fire and discovered the body?"

"Well, the smoke was first seen by Mr. Pounder, the assistant to Mr. Paul Merriweather, the Senior Warden. Mr. Merriweather automatically became the Master Mason upon Withermew's death. They both came running to the office of Dr. Withermew to find the library burning and the fire creeping around through the open doorway to his office, what with the papers being blown by the wind because of the open windows. They discovered the dead body of Dr. Withermew."

The detective opened his eyes and leaned forward once more. "Did they see anything else?"

"Yes. Before the fire forced them back, they saw two people running away in opposite directions."

"Two people you say?"

"One they saw out the window was already heading out of the courtyard. But they both swear they recognized him as Randall Tobias, a Mason member of their Brotherhood. He being the one they suspect of being the murderer."

"And why do they suspect him of being the murderer?"

"Well, sir, they said they saw him running away fast from the side office door."

"I see," Holmes said, "the murderer would have to be the one running the fastest." He shook his head at the assumption of the two witnesses. "I assume that you have the Yard out looking for this Tobias fellow?"

"We are." Hopkins flipped open his small notebook and began going through the pages quickly. Finding what he was seeking, he said, "He's of average height with thick mutton chops and receding, curly brown hair."

"And so is half of London," Holmes said. "And where was the body in relation to this Tobias?"

"The body was at the opposite side of the office where the door opens up to the library," Hopkins said. "Tobias had already gone out the opposite door about three hundred feet away and into the courtyard leading to the street."

Holmes shook his head slightly and raised his finger to his lips. "And what of this second fellow?"

"They saw him just leaving the library at the opposite end of the floor."

"And what did this fellow look like?" Holmes asked.

Hopkins consulted his notebook once more.

"His back was to them, and he was just one step ahead of the flames. Plus he had a cloak and hood drawn up tight about his head and face."

Holmes arched an eyebrow. "Is that all they recall?"

"No. They said he was a fairly good-sized chap and moved with considerable adroitness."

"Once again," Holmes said, his tone laced with sarcasm, "that narrows the field of potential suspects considerably."

"He had just begun running away when they arrived. He went the other way from his accomplice."

"He was not an accomplice, Hopkins, but rather a second criminal who had come late to the scene of the crime. And I would further say that this second man was also the arsonist and murderer."

"How would you know that?" the Inspector asked incredulously.

"Quite simply," Holmes replied. "The two suspects arrived at separate times and from different directions. One was not concerned in the least with disguising his identity, while the second one took great pains to conceal his face, indicating that he had knowledge of the more serious nature of the crime that had been committed. If this Tobias fellow had committed the murder, wouldn't he have been more diligent about concealing his identity?"

Hopkins pursed his lips. "Yes, I suppose so, when you put it that way."

"What was the condition of Withermews's room after the fire?"

Hopkins paged through his notebook again. "His office was barely touched by the fire. Battalion Chief Polk said the fire was started in the doorway between the office and the library. I really don't know the reason for that. Could be from some candles being knocked over and setting the old books ablaze. But the two open windows blew some of the flames from the burning books into the office and started burning some papers in Withermew's space. That's what pushed Merriweather and Pounder back."

"Were they able to determine if anything had been taken from the office? Anything of value?"

The inspector paged through the notebook once more. The man was obviously most sagacious about documentation.

"The new Grand Master Mason did report one thing missing," he said. "Withermew had a wall safe. It was wide open and it was empty."

"And what, pray tell, was in it?" Holmes placed his fingers in front of his face in the shape of a steeple once more.

Again, Hopkins consulted his notes, and then looked up. "A small metal chest that may have been in the safe."

An eyebrow rose on the detective's forehead. "*May* have been?"

Hopkins gave an emphatic nod. "That's what they assumed. They weren't sure if it was in the safe or hidden somewhere around the office. Mr. Merriweather was upset by Dr. Withermew's death, but seemed more concerned about a cache of papers he said was held in that metal box. He and Mr. Pounder were searching frantically for it, tearing the place apart, but had no luck in locating it. He and his assistant went through the ashes of the library looking for a chest but to no avail. When I inquired as to the nature of the papers for my report, he grew rather agitated and said it was private Mason business and would remain such. But he demanded that it be recovered unopened by Scotland Yard or there would be consequences."

"A private Mason matter," I said. "Who are they to dictate terms to the authorities?"

Holmes said nothing.

"That's why I've come to you, Mr. Holmes," Hopkins said. "I've got a suspicious fire at the Masonic Lodge involving very important Masons and the death of the prominent Dr. Alfred Withermew, and now a missing metal strong box with secret papers. I don't know exactly where to start. This is the biggest case I've ever been assigned, and I know I need your assistance on this. Can you assist me?"

Holmes didn't answer immediately. Instead, he picked up the pipe again, tested the contents of the bowl with his index finger, and then reached into the pocket of his gown for a match. "Why do you need my help, Hopkins? It seems as if you only have to round up this Tobias fellow and locate the hooded man and the case is solved." Holmes struck the match and held the flame over the top of the bowl.

An expression of desperation overtook Hopkins's face. "But I have no way of figuring out who killed Dr. Withermew, this Tobias or the hooded man. The fire took away all clues."

Holmes continued to puff on the pipe as the shreds of tobacco turned red.

"And I'm in the dark as to what I'm looking for in the missing papers in the metal box," Hopkins continued. "How am I supposed to find something if I don't know what it is that I'm looking for?"

Holmes blew out a cloud of smoke and fixed the man with an intense stare.

"And what's the rest of it?" he asked.

Hopkins crunched his lips together and looked askance. "Well, my Chief Constable is a Senior Deacon in the Masons. When I was handed this assignment I was told right out that I had to solve it as quickly and as discreetly as possible. There is to be no press or spotlight shown on this matter. And I had better solve it with all haste."

Holmes smirked. "And he anointed you and you alone with this task? You must be held in high esteem in his eyes."

The expression of doubt lingered over the Inspector as he slowly shook his head.

"Or is it that yours is just the first head that will roll if this case is not solved quickly and to his satisfaction?" Holmes said. "Not very sporting of him, is it, Watson?"

"Hardly," I replied, my hopes again buoying that my friend would once more become engaged with a new mystery that would occupy his most brilliant mind.

He turned to me. "So what do you think we have, old boy? An arson? A burglary? A murder?"

"All three, from the sound of it," I answered.

"Indeed." He drew in some smoke from the pipe and blew it out a second later without removing the stem. It does sounds a bit intriguing. Either way, I would find it a bit amusing to dabble in the inner workings of such a secretive organization."

An expression of relief and delight seemed to overtake the inspector.

"Then you'll help me, Mr. Holmes?"

"I shall," Holmes said. "You certainly have a momentous task laid out before you. You appear to have two thieves running in different directions. Secret papers that are more important than a man's life. The only suspect is a fellow Mason who runs very fast. Am I forgetting anything?"

"The unfortunate fire in the Masonic Lodge," I said.

"Ah, yes, Watson, very good. I'm not sure that Scotland Yard is equipped to take on the Masons. What say you, Doctor? Are you ready to put out a fire?"

"Why who knows, Holmes, perhaps this fire might end up being started by the Devil himself, as you speculated," said I.

"Very well," my companion said. "Allow us time to get our coats and we shall join you in a cab and go to the Mason Lodge presently."

He stood up abruptly and moved towards the door, pausing to stoop down and pick up the sodden newspaper pages. He opened the door and shouted, "Oh, Mrs. Hudson."

A few moments later our kindly landlady appeared at our door.

Holmes handed her the wadded up paper, smiled, and said, "Dr. Watson and I must go out. If you would be so kind, when a Mr. Judstonberry comes calling please collect thirty pounds and when it is safely placed in your apron pocket tell him to get his ring back from his fiancée immediately because by the end of the week she will be in Lisbon or quite possibly Madrid. And she will most assuredly be there without him."

The old lady's mouth formed into an O and she nodded.

He grabbed his coat, top hat and walking stick. "Come, Watson, we are off to the temple to see some Masons."

CHAPTER 2
THE MASONIC LODGE

The four-wheeler pulled away from the curb with a jerk and we were off across north London to the Masonic Lodge. The thunder still peeled in the distance with ever lessening flashes of meager lightning attempting to scratch through the grey morning sky. As we settled in, Holmes turned to Hopkins and said," What else can you tell me about the fire?"

Hopkins turned slightly toward my friend with a look of satisfaction on his face for being asked to share his knowledge on the subject with the detective.

"Once I was able to gain entry to the office and the library, I availed my-self of the expertise of Battalion Chief Oscar Polk," he said. "He is a most meticulous fellow whose reports read like your accounts of Mr. Holmes cases, Dr. Watson. He captures every detail and his descriptions of the event make you feel like you were actually there in the fire itself."

I felt a slight flush of embarrassment. "Well, I do try to put a bit of detail into my writing."

"Is it your conjecture, inspector," Holmes interjected, "that it was one of dear Watson's readers who used the lurid accounts of our adventures to start the fire to warm his hands?"

Both Hopkins and I ignored Holmes's jest.

"So I take it that Polk had no problem in securing the scene?" said I.

"None, whatsoever." Hopkins wrinkled his brow into a commiserating expression. "I found out later that he's a member of the Masons, and a rather prominent one at that. I overheard one of the big wigs, a treasurer or some such, ask about Polk's father, who apparently is a rather well-to-do business man and a Mason, too. It doesn't hurt to be connected."

"And the fire?" my companion pressed on, seemingly totally uninter-ested in the Polk's position within the Masons. "What did the illustrious Chief Polk find?"

Hopkins raised his eyebrows and shrugged, as if he were reestablishing his train of thought. "He wasn't sure yet if it was accidental, or if there was a scuffle."

"A scuffle?" Holmes asked.

"Yes. You see, a candelabra was knocked over in the hallway between the office and the library where the body was found."

"And is that what started the blaze?" I inquired.

Again, Hopkins shrugged. "That would be my guess. What else could it have been?"

"Well," I offered, playing a bit of the Devil's advocate, "who's to say that it didn't get knocked over by someone who saw the initial blaze and fled?"

Hopkins lifted his hand and stroked his chin with his fingers.

"I hadn't thought of that," he said.

I felt a surge of satisfaction at having already raised a substantial inves-tigative question.

"What do you think, Holmes?" I asked.

"That it remains to be seen," Holmes said. "We shall certainly ascertain more when we arrive at the Temple. In the meantime, is there anything more that can be said about these Masons?"

"Nothing more than their leaders are all men of influence and high standing in society," Hopkins said. "Their senior leadership reads like the society page of the upper class."

"I might be able to help you there, Holmes," I said. "My late Mary's second cousin was a member of the Masons."

"But aren't they sworn to secrecy?" Hopkins asked.

"Most certainly," I replied, and then smiled. "But he had a fondness for sherry and, after a significant bit of imbibing, he had a tendency to ramble on a bit concerning the secrets about a club whose existence is built upon secrecy."

"Indeed," Holmes said. "Do go on, old fellow."

"Well," I continued. "It's a well known fact that the Masons claim to be the oldest fraternal organization in England, and they started with the guilds of stone masons in the fourteenth century." I took out my pipe, held it out the window, and tapped the residual ash from the bowl. "They profess to be non-religious and non-political in nature. Popular legend has it that their lineage traces back to the Knights Templar, the Crusaders who were once the most powerful force in medieval Europe. Like the Knights Templars, their meetings are cloaked in the utmost secrecy." I pulled out my tobacco pouch and began packing the bowl. "Thus, their penchant for secret handshakes and passwords, and the reliance on secret symbols."

"I know about those," Hopkins said. "The stone mason's square and compass."

"Quite," I said, a bit irritated at being interrupted. I struck a match and held the flame over the top of the bowl and gingerly puffed its contents to a small ember.

"When he was drunk," I said. "Mary's cousin, Freddie, liked to boast that he was a Mason because they were at the forefront of knowledge, although you couldn't tell it from old Freddie boy. He said technically they met in a Temple of Philosophy where they swear allegiance to one Grand Lodge that controls all the other separate lodges."

"He seemed to have quite a loose set of lips," Holmes said.

I blew out a bit of smoke. "They truly are a brotherhood in the most literal sense of the word." I allowed myself a trace of a smile. "Of course, no women are allowed to join their ranks. All of their meetings are very private and sworn to absolute secrecy."

"Unless one has imbibed too much sherry," Holmes said.

"Yes," I said. "They're governed by a Masonic Master then Senior Wardens I believe."

"A senior warden?" Hopkins asked. "What's that?"

"It's one who takes over when the Master is gone," Holmes said. "Then the others formulate a line of succession."

I was momentarily surprised at the correctness of his statement, but then again, Holmes had a tremendous knowledge of virtually everything.

"You're absolutely correct, Holmes," I said, resuming. "From the stories that Freddie told me, their members include magistrates, governors, justices, wealthy merchants, high-placed civil servants and the like. It sounded to me as if they weren't keeping to their sworn oath of eschewing the political."

"That much is obvious," Holmes said.

"I just had a thought," Hopkins said, "what if they don't let us back into the temple because we're not Masons?"

Holmes smiled. "I'm sure you'll think of something in that event, Inspector."

With that, the cab took a sharp right up Balcombe Street and we continued on our way to the Masonic Temple building.

Holmes swore that he had never seen so much traffic on London streets as he did this morning. I must admit, I tended to agree with him, for it seemed that for every lane we turned down we found ourselves behind delivery wagons or double-decker trolleys. I smoked up the entire contents of the pipe I'd packed, and was halfway through another when we arrived and the slot on the rear top of the cab slid open. The driver thrust his head in front of it to announce that we were at the cross section of Whitmore Way North West and Stockwood Exchange. I extinguished my pipe and took a moment to take out my pocket watch and glance at it. It was half past ten, and luckily the rainy drizzle had abated, although there were numerous puddles of standing water peppering the cobblestones.

Moments later, we three stood in front of the squared off point of the entrance to the Masonic Lodge. The impressive building's outer facade resembled that of a temple. It was three stories tall and over one block long. The triangular shape stood out boldly, its facade adorned with four two-story marble Doric pillars anchored to its brownstone. There was a broad, semi-circular stairway in the front, and centered perfectly between the two pillars in the middle was a ten-foot brass door inlaid with the Mason's builder's square and compass. It was flanked by cathedral windows covered by thick, red velvet curtains on the inside. The building's cornerstone read *1768*.

The street in front of the Temple was congested with dozens of business men meeting on corners and a ragged news boy selling what's left of his *Daily Mirrors*. My companion stood there taking in the scene quite intently, and then moved up the steps to a pair of gentlemen who had just greeted each other. The detective doffed his hat and began a conversation with the men. After several gestures, he bowed, shook their hands and rejoined us at the curb.

I thought nothing of it as I was engaged with the sight that greeted me as I glanced up at the top of the building and I spied along the triangular base of its enormous roof line the words carved in stone: *The Free Masons Build Their Temples Among Nations and in the Hearts of Men.*

I wondered if they carved *Murder* in there also.

We stepped through the large brass door and found ourselves in a small, windowless anti-chamber lit only by two brass braziers standing four feet off the floor; the glow from its embers gave the room a queer reddish tint. Two strategically placed vents kept the air flowing smoothly through the room so that there was hardly a hint of charcoal in the air. There we were greeted by a rather large and wide man, very nicely dressed, but he was an obvious obstacle to further advancement.

"May I help you, gentlemen?" his voice echoed in the tiny enclosure.

"Yes, Scotland Yard Inspector Stanley Hopkins to see Mr. Merriweather." His voice was sharp and crisp.

"Are you a Mason, sir?"

"No." Hopkins replied sternly. "I'm from Scotland Yard."

The enormous man's visage hardened.

"I really don't care who you're with. Only Masons are allowed in the Temple."

The Inspector quickly took his badge out of his jacket pocket and held it up in front of the big man's face. "This is official Yard business and you will step aside," he said forcefully. "Now."

"Get that blasted thing away from my face," the huge man growled.

"Maybe I can be of some help, Inspector," Holmes said stepping in front of Hopkins.

The brute stared at him. "Listen, governor, no one gets in here unless they're a Mason."

"Why, of course, my friend. I wouldn't have it any other way." With that Holmes extended his right hand palm upward, and thrust it out before him.

The human blockade looked down, paused for a few moments, then gripped my companion's open palm and they shook hands. There was a momentary look of astonishment on the brute's face, and then he repeated

"Get that blasted thing out of my face."

the gesture with his own hand.

Holmes placed his open left hand over the top of his palm, and then quickly elevated his hand to just under his chin. His right hand was then thrust forward with his thumb and little finger extended. The three other fingers were curled back.

The large man extended his fist in a similar fashion and the two men's little fingers intertwined. The tips of their thumbs touched like the beaks of two enamored birds, and then their hands disengaged.

I was astounded, as was Hopkins. I had no idea that Holmes knew the secret handshake. For a brief moment I wondered if he was a member of the Masons and had kept it secret from me all these years.

"I would like to formally introduce myself," he said. "I'm Sherlock Holmes. Please direct us to the Master Mason's office."

The huge man looked solemn as he turned and held the door open.

"Oh," Holmes said, gesturing toward Hopkins and me. "These gentlemen are coming with me as guests."

The big brute's lips pursed and he gave a curt nod.

As we followed our large guide through the corridors inside the oak paneled walls, I leaned forward and whispered into my companion's ear. "Holmes, are you a Mason?"

The hint of a smile tickled his mouth and he shook his head.

The answer furthered my astonishment.

I glanced forward at the massive guardian. He hadn't seemed to hear us. I kept my voice at a whisper. "Then how the Devil did you learn that elaborate ritual? That confounded handshake?"

"Tidbits picked up on one of my many treks about our metropolis," he said.

I was once again reminded of my dear companion's remarkable ability to see something once and to retain it forthwith.

"Imagine," I said, still using *sotto voce*. "A simple handshake and we've gained entrance to the inner sanctum. But how did you know he'd fall for it."

"I didn't, Watson. But it seemed a less cumbersome method than having to remove him by force." His smile grew wider. "One of the benefits of dealing with an organization that prides itself on upholding secrecy, and requires such elaborate reciprocity, is that many of the members are unsure of the other's identity. I recalled that the Mason's relied on secret greetings to acknowledge each other, and when our mammoth friend said that only Masons could be allowed in, I decided that I would become a Mason."

I glanced behind us to assure myself that Hopkins was out of earshot as well. "How the deuce did you suddenly become a Mason?"

"It was merely a matter of repeating the gestures that I observed several of the businessmen giving each other outside of the temple when we arrived. When we exited the cab, I noticed that when the men greeted each other they cupped their thumbs into their palms and then shook hands with the thumb tucked inward, not outward encircling the other fellow's hand. I decided to test my theory on the two gentlemen I encountered outside on the steps when I approached them and asked for directions. Neither one flinched when I exchanged that handshake. They just smiled knowingly, acknowledging me as a fellow Mason."

"Amazing, Holmes. Simply amazing."

"Hold your accolades, old chum," he whispered back. "I fear we may have one more obstacle to cross."

I looked down the hall and saw another Masonic guardian, as impressive specimen as the first, standing up ahead. His brow knitted as he saw us approaching.

"Quickly, Watson," Holmes said. "To which lodge did your late wife's cousin belong?"

I thought for a moment, and then whispered my reply.

"Excuse me," the second man said, glaring at the big fellow who'd escorted us. "I don't recall seeing any of you at this temple before."

I looked through the open door and saw a large, opulent meeting room its chairs neatly stacked facing a small raised platform.

"To which lodge are you members?"

"That would be the one on Queen Anne's Street," Holmes replied.

I quickly added the address of that lodge having it been burnt into my memory by cousin Freddie's incessant ramblings.

"God's Temple on earth," I blurted out. "Or at best, one of his magnificent waiting rooms."

With this pronouncement the second behemoth smiled.

"Ah, yes. Very well." He stepped aside and extended his arm, ushering us forward.

A moment later we were standing in the doorway of a rather grand office decorated with dozens of brass, gold, and wood-carved Masonic symbols of architect's squares and compasses. Several shelves held builder's plumbs, all taking measurements of phantom constructs far beyond the confines of the room. There were countless silver and gold triangles with the all-seeing eye emblazoned in their center, the Eye of Providence staring out, giving one the feeling that they were watching everything going on throughout the temple and beyond.

One entire wall was adorned with portraits of distinguished men in their finest wares, looking regal and imposing at whoever was viewing them. Also posted on the walls between the paintings were gold anchors, Masonic gavels and the Masonic Blazing Star. Around the room were several teak credenzas holding brilliant replicas in every size of the Ark of the Covenant. I recalled from Freddie's drunken ravings that it was an important symbol in the Masonic traditions. Lastly, there was a virtual forest of small wooden or gold-plated or silver-edged representations of Acacia trees filling every space left available.

Holmes had apparently been studying my curious and fascinated inspection and leaned close to whisper in my ear. "The Acacia tree is the Masonic symbol of immortality."

I was again astounded at the depth of his knowledge, and that he'd so cleverly read my thoughts once more. I was glad as well, that I had paid some attention to cousin Freddie's' tedious prattle.

From behind a large oak desk a slightly overweight figure, immaculately dressed as if he were a trustee of the Bank of England, stepped out to greet us. His mane of white hair, strong nose and mutton chop sideburns only further added to his distinguished regal visage.

"Fellow members here to see you, Grand Master," our guide announced.

"Gentlemen, please, come in." He extended his hand to us and smiled. "Inspector Hopkins, isn't it? I didn't know that you were a Mason."

"Why," Hopkins started to say.

Standing behind him, Holmes reached over and pinched the man's leg.

Hopkins immediately coughed, and then recovered quite nicely.

"How nice to see you again, as well, Mr. Merriweather," Hopkins spoke rather quickly, apparently realizing that he now had to keep up this new posture as a Masonic member. "These are my companions, Mr. Sherlock Holmes and Dr. John Watson."

"Ah, a Scotland Yard inspector, a prominent physician and the renowned Sherlock Holmes, all members of the Brotherhood. How splendid."

"Hardly," Holmes muttered.

"What did he say?" asked Merriweather.

"He said heavenly," I quickly replied.

Without any further ado, Merriweather dismissed our large guide. As he left the office, his place was taken by a tall, bald headed man with a thick beard, who, because of his somewhat gruff exterior, did not quite fit into the mold of a business type.

"This is my assistant, Mr. Pounder," the Grand Master said.

Hopkins nodded and said, "Yes, I recognize you from last night. You were the one who tried to prevent me from gaining entrance to the crime scene."

Pounder's impassive face showed no reaction.

Merriweather cleared his throat.

"Let me be the first to apologize for Mr. Pounder's actions of last evening." He glanced over at the bald-headed man with a reproachful eye. "As I'm sure you're aware, he was just following Masonic tradition according to our by-laws." He paused a moment and raised an eyebrow. "Being a Mason, you know that outsiders aren't allowed into the temple at any time. You should have identified yourself as a fellow Mason right away." His brow knitted once more. "And, by the way, why didn't you?"

"If he is a Mason," Pounder said.

Holmes immediately stepped in.

"And you surely recognize the stress that Inspector Hopkins was under coming to a place as sacred to him as this Masonic Lodge in the middle of the night, observing it on fire and trying to contain the area and keep the crime scene free from contamination while observing and cataloguing every sight and sound in the chaos going about him."

Merriweather seemed momentarily taken aback.

"Such a monumental task," Holmes continued, "was in no small measure an arduous one. He was entering the Lodge, as was his right and duty as a Mason, and also as an officer of the law, trying to determine the cause of the fire and the nature of how Dr. Withermew came to meet his unfortunate end. He can be forgiven for not having identified himself to your assistant here that he was a Mason, now can he not?"

There was no immediate response, and then Merriweather emitted a muffled grunt of assent. Holmes seemed pleased with his explanation.

Hopkins took advantage of the pause to get right down to business. "And now, good sir, will you kindly take us to the library and the office of the late Dr. Withermew?"

With that we all moved back into the exquisite wood paneled passageways, past sitting rooms and more offices. Soon, we were at the charred confines of the library and its connecting anterooms. True to their reputation as master craftsmen, the area was almost completely cleared and all burnt books and furniture had already been removed. A small crew of workers was gingerly disassembling two massive bookcases from the connecting wall between the office and library. Merriweather spoke to them and they put down their tools and left the area.

"I hope that you find this useful, gentlemen?" the Grand Mason offered.

"Useful in the fact that any and all clues have been removed." Holmes huffed in disgust.

Merriweather and Pounder exchanged glances. It seemed a bit of unspoken conversation was going on between the two of them.

Hopkins produced his steadfast notebook once again and consulted it. "Chief Polk determined that the fire began right here at the last stack of books next to the opening to the office. There were two sets of candelabras found here."

Holmes dropped to one knee and scraped the floor, pulling up slivers of wax underneath his fingernail.

"Hardly a clever space to start a fire if your purpose was to burn down an entire room," he said. "This fire was accidental; or rather it would appear that it was the byproduct of a struggle taking place here with Dr. Withermew meeting this Tobias or his hooded assailant. And this is where the body was found, correct?"

The detective went on not waiting for Hopkins' verbal affirmation.

"I can only assume that Withermew fell back into the office area and the books in the end bookcase caught fire instantly." He rose and strode about the room. "With the breeze from the storm outside blowing through the open windows, it fanned the flames back into the office, effectively cutting off the purported hooded man from gaining access to Withermew's office."

Holmes stepped carefully back in a wide circle to where the bookshelf stood, now half disassembled. "Can anyone tell me if the books in here that were consumed by the fire were still on their shelves or were they scattered about on the floor?"

The question seemed to take the group by surprise as no one spoke up immediately.

"Well, surely someone must recall where the majority of books were lying when the fire was put out." Holmes raised a querulous eyebrow as his stare went from Hopkins to Merriweather to Pounder. "That is why things should not be moved at the scene of the crime," he added.

"To my best recollection," Hopkins said after a slight cough and stutter, "the books were scattered all across the floor. I remember walking across the charred spines and pages of many old books thinking what a shame it was that—"

"Thank you, Hopkins," Holmes said, interrupting him. "You are to be commended. Your eye for detail has come in quite handily."

Merriweather cleared his throat. "Yes, I concur. I do believe they were scattered about."

Holmes turned his gaze to Pounder, who shrugged.

"Scattered about, they was," he said.

"Thank you," my companion added, the hint of sarcasm imbued in his tone.

"Why is that important, Mr. Holmes?" Hopkins asked.

The detective canted his head and once again raised an eyebrow slightly. "It is important because it shows me that the assailant spent what little time he had left rifling through the books. He was obviously looking for something, possibly papers, hidden within."

Merriweather, Pounder, and Hopkins had expressions of complete befuddlement.

Holmes heaved a sigh.

"If the books had been burnt while sitting next to each other on their shelves," he said, "that would be the normal progression of the fire. But since they were ripped from their resting space and then discarded with such abandon that it caused them to be burned while scattered haphazard on the floor meant that they were handled before they became ash."

Once again, Merriweather, Pounder, and Hopkins had looks of astonishment.

Holmes, however, advanced toward the wall where a blackened metallic door about the size of a horizontal portrait was recessed into the solid wall.

"This is the wall safe you mentioned?" Holmes asked Hopkins.

"Now see here," Merriweather interrupted. "There was nothing of monetary value in that safe. No money a'tall."

"No money," Holmes said. "But a metal dispatch box that you and your confederate, Mr. Pounder, spent a considerable amount of time searching for last night."

Merriweather blubbered something unintelligible about the confusion at the scene.

Holmes stopped his protestation with a sharp glance.

"Obviously," he said, "there was something of value in it that caused a man his life. Would you like to share with us what the exact contents were?"

"Why…" Merriweather's lips drew together like the purse strings of a miser's wallet. "I haven't the foggiest. Why would I? It wasn't my office."

"And it's none of your business, either," Pounder added.

Holmes stared at the man for a solid ten beats of the clock, and then flared his nostrils in apparent disgust as he lifted one finger to his lips.

"Let us look at what we know for certain. Two men broke in here last night, a man was murdered, both thieves were looking for something, perhaps the same thing, and we have to assume it was the contents of the metal box. And the safe in the office was emptied. Now, who found it before the fire chased them out?"

"That is why I am glad that the police have asked you to become involved in this matter, Mr. Holmes," Merriweather said. "Your reputation for solving crimes and keeping secrets safe is of the utmost importance in this case."

"And I," Hopkins said, "am very glad as well, Mr. Holmes."

The detective took in a deep breath, and then allowed himself a brief smile. "Well, any time I am able to be of help to Scotland Yard, I am most happy to do so. Now, I must first know a few more details. Perhaps you will enlighten me as to what it was that Dr. Withermew might have had in this metal box that the two intruders would be so readily disposed to kill him to acquire it?"

"What more do you need to know, Mr. Holmes?" Merriweather said. "We have identified the killer as Randall Tobias, regrettably a fellow Mason."

"We need to find him and ascertain if he stole the metal box from the late Dr. Withermew," Pounder added.

"And what would be in that metal box?" the detective asked.

"We already told you that we don't know," Pounder said. "Didn't we?"

"Indeed you did." My companion turned slowly to face the Grand Master. "My dear fellow, I do not attempt to solve a case with only half the information. I must have all the facts if I am to proceed. One does not milk a cow with only half a bucket. Now, what did Dr. Withermew have in his possession that was worth killing for?"

Merriweather stood silent for several moments.

"Please do not insult my intelligence with any more preposterous statements about you not knowing the contents of the box," Holmes said.

The other man's mouth worked, as if he was chewing the detective's words, and then he said, "All right, perhaps I do have an idea."

"An idea?" Holmes chortled. "I asked you not to insult my intelligence, sir."

Merriweather's face reddened and he shook his head. "All right. But I cannot divulge the exact nature of the contents to you. Only members of the Royal Arch Masons of the Lodges are privileged to know that information."

"Then the members of the Royal Arch of Masons can keep that information," Holmes answered. "Come, Watson, we are done here." With that he abruptly turned away and headed towards the direction from which we had just come.

"Mr. Holmes, please," Hopkins implored.

"If I am not to be trusted with all the particulars of this case, then I am wasting my time, and I have a distinct aversion to doing so."

"You can't just leave," Merriweather bellowed. "I won't allow it."

"Let him go," Pounder said; his voice an angry shout.

Holmes seemed unaffected by the other men's bluster. He continued his trek toward the door. I fell into step behind him.

"Best of luck to you all," Holmes said. "Let the Masons chase this fugitive with their secrets with their trowels and cement."

We were a step away from the door when Merriweather called out. "Wait!"

I caught the slightest hint of a smirk cross my friend's lips.

We paused and waited.

"My apologies, Mr. Holmes," said Merriweather finally. "If you must know what we hope to regain, then I believe a man of your sterling reputation and integrity can be trusted without hesitation. But this must be kept to the smallest circle possible."

"I can assure you that neither I nor Dr. Watson will ever speak a word of it to anyone who does not need to know. Now, Inspector Hopkins, if you would be so kind as to leave us here alone with the Grand Master, we can proceed with our investigation."

"What?" Hopkins said. "But I'm in charge of this investigation."

"Not anymore," Merriweather said. "I'll speak to your superiors at the Yard about that."

The police inspector frowned, and then said with the tone of dejection, "If you insist."

"We most certainly do. Thank you. We'll catch up with you, and Mr. Pounder back at Mr. Merriweather's office."

It was Pounder's turn to appear angry and dejected.

Hopkins left with Mr. Pounder by his side.

CHAPTER 3
THE SECRET ANTHOLOGY

Shortly, Mr. Merriweather, Holmes and I were alone in the library. I leaned heavily to one side using my cane for support as we had been standing in one spot for a protracted period of time and there were no chairs. Holmes recognized this immediately and suggested that we move further into the room to where the fire had not damaged the furniture and allowed the three of us to sit comfortably in chairs.

"First of all," Merriweather said. "I must ask that what I'm about to tell you remains in the strictest confidence. It's not to be bandied about in some lurid penny dreadful, Dr. Watson. May I have your word on that?"

Holmes glanced at me, and I gave a quick nod. The detective turned back to Merriweather.

"You have our word," he said.

Merriweather sat and brought his hand to his mouth. After a bit of contemplation, he spoke. "I suppose that I should start at the beginning. A short history lesson is best."

"By all means," Holmes said. "Please proceed."

He crossing his legs and brought his hand to his chin, giving me a view of his classic profile.

"Have you ever heard of the Iron Crown of Lombardy?" Merriweather began.

Holmes said nothing, but the name was a bit familiar to me.

"Yes," I said. "I believe it was used in the coronation of the Holy Roman Emperors, was it not?"

"Yes, Doctor," Merriweather said. "But it means so much more in the annals of the Catholic Church. It is one of the oldest blessed insignias in Christendom. It was commissioned by Saint Helena, the mother of Constantine the Great." He closed his eyes, as if conjuring up the image. "It was a circlet of gold and twenty-two jewels fitted onto a silver band inlaid in iron. And in the iron was imbedded a nail from the True Cross, the cross upon which Christ was crucified. It is an Arma Christi; one of the Instruments of the Passion."

"That makes it quite a holy relic, doesn't it?" said I.

"Very true. It was so revered that it was used to coronate Holy Roman emperors such as Charlemagne, all the way to Napoleon." He paused and took in another deep breath. "But here's where the story gets a bit more tangled in a web of intrigue."

Holmes, without moving his head, darted his eyes to stare at the Grand Master, then quickly returned to staring off to the side. "Do go on."

"According to tradition, before she died, Saint Helena bequeathed the Iron Crown to Pope Gregory the Great. Years later, Pope Gregory gave it to the princess of Lombardy. From there it was donated to the Cathedral in Monza, outside of Milan, where it supposedly lies today."

"But we know better," Holmes said. "Do we not?"

Merriweather compressed his lips.

"Well," he continued, "there is another tradition that says Saint Helena gave the Iron Crown to Emperor Theodosius, who kept the crown in Constantinople. It resided there until 1204, and the siege of Constantinople by the Crusaders." He stopped and took in another deep breath. "Here's where this account becomes a tad murky. The crown disappears from all historical records. Legend has it that the Iron Crown was taken from Constantinople by the Templars and brought back to England as a spoil of war."

Merriweather leaned back in his chair and looked up as if trying to remember the story with all its detail.

"That is until September 27, 1307 when the writings of Sir John Randolph Secret of Sussex mention a votive crown of iron with twenty-some gemstones being hidden away after the arrest of the Knights Templars in France and England on Friday, October 13, 1307. King Phillip and King Edward II were jealous of the Templars power and wealth and holdings, so they persecuted them on false charges and confiscated their land, belongings and holy relics."

"So which tradition is correct, Mr. Merriweather?" Holmes said, straightening up in his chair.

Merriweather licked his lips. "This second Iron Crown has to be the one. It has to be." There was a gleam of fanaticism in his eyes. "The one taken from Constantinople by the Knights Templars. Surely, Saint Helena wouldn't have given the original crown away to someone who would take it from its rightful place, Constantinople. It has to be the one given to Theodosius, the one liberated by the Templars, brought back to England and hidden away when the Templars were persecuted in 1307."

"And how would the Masons know about this Templar treasure?" I asked.

Merriweather directed his stare at me. "The Free Masons were founded upon the Templars, Dr. Watson. The Templars who escaped the wrath of Britain's King Edward II still felt the need for a society to protect their fellow man. In the late fourteenth century, the stone masons had begun forming guilds because of the holy fervor in building cathedrals all over England. These guilds were joined and organized by the old Templars. The Masons adopted the ranks of Grand Masters and Wardens from the Templars, the secret handshakes and rituals and initiations. The Free Masons owe a lot to the Templars." His brow knitted once again in confusion. "But if you're Masons, as you claim, you should know this."

Before I could respond, Holmes spoke.

"I see," he said, canting his head to one side. "And what of this Iron Crown that was hidden away?"

"It is the great honor of our Lodge to be the keeper of some of the texts of Templar writings from that period of time when the Templars were hiding their spoils of war from the Holy Land and the Ottoman Empire. It is a series of short epistles, no more than twenty pages that was put together and called *The Secret Anthology*, after Sir John Randolph Secret. Unfortunately, they are written in Latin and a cryptic code that no one has been able to decipher for centuries."

"A cryptic code?" I said.

"Yes," Merriweather said. "Of course, the codes for some of the lesser relics were deciphered and retrieved. But the Iron Crown, the most precious relic man can think of holding in his hands, remains forever hidden."

"And," Holmes asked, "this anthology is where, exactly?"

Merriweather sighed. "That is the problem. The bound papers were being kept in a metal box in Dr. Withermew's office. I assumed they were in his safe. But they were not there. I searched his desk and drawers and his shelves. Nothing. Then in his books. Behind them. In them. Nothing. In desperation we searched the library, hoping the copies weren't burnt to ashes."

"The copies?" Holmes said sharply.

"Ah, yes, the copies. I forgot to tell you about the copies." Merriweather's face creased as if pressured by an unseen weight. "He kept two sets of copies in a wooden treasure chest, his idea of a jest, on the first shelf here in the library. The precept was that to hide something in such an obvious place, in plain sight, would be the safest procedure." He turned and gestured toward the empty wall. "As you can see, there is nothing left of the first shelf."

There seemed to be no breath left in Merriweather.

"Who knew about the existence of this Anthology?" the detective asked.

"Just Dr. Withermew, myself and the past Grand Master."

"Not your assistant, Mr. Pounder?"

"No. He just knows that we are looking for important Mason papers."

"And who might this past Grand Master be?"

"Pastor Ezra Thaddeus. But he is hospitalized and rather ill."

"Well," Holmes sprang to his feet. "Now we have some additional fodder for our mystery. Where is the Secret Anthology, if it isn't here? How did our two thieves know of the existence of this Anthology, and was that the subject of their break in?" He paused and glanced my way. "And what good is it to them if it's in Latin and it can't be deciphered?"

I had been wondering the same thing.

Holmes strolled over to the burnt wall once again, studied it, and then turned back toward Merriweather. "Thank you, sir, for being so forthright. I know this must have been difficult for you, but now that I have the complete picture I can begin our search for this Tobias, this second hooded fellow, and the Iron Crown Anthology."

Merriweather's face was a portrait of anxiety.

"Do you think you can find it, Mr. Holmes?"

The detective raised an imperious eyebrow.

"I shall do my best," he said.

CHAPTER 4
THE BATTALION CHIEF

Merriweather led us back through the temple to his office where we rejoined Hopkins and Pounder. The latter shot an intense stare at us, and then focused on Merriweather. I imagined that there would be much friction to come in the great hall once we departed.

Holmes seemed oblivious to the possible tempest, however. As we walked, Hopkins attempted to interrogate us about what Merriweather had told us in private.

"What did he say to you?"

"Nothing of importance to you," Holmes said. "It was private concern he wished to voice."

"A private concern?" The inspector appeared befuddled.

"Quite," Holmes said. "And now, inspector, we must beg your leave for a bit."

"My leave?" The space between his brows knitted. "But I thought we were working on this together."

"We are," Holmes said. "However, we have something of paramount importance to attend to at present."

I wasn't certain to what Holmes was referring, but remained silent. My question was answered forthwith.

"I don't understand, Mr. Holmes," Hopkins said.

Holmes ignored the question and turned to me.

"Watson," he said, "could I trouble you for the time?"

I took out my pocket watch, flipped open the lid, and glanced down at the hands.

"Why, it's three minutes after noon," I said, suddenly feeling the pangs of hunger gripping at my innards.

Holmes smiled. "And that answers your question, inspector. It is time for lunch, and the good doctor here will tell you that the mind works best when the stomach is not empty."

Hopkins's mouth was momentarily agape, and then he recovered.

"Why, yes," he said. "I am feeling rather hungry at that."

Holmes waved at an approaching hansom.

"I would ask you to join us," he said, "but we're expecting a special visitor at our lodgings. Shall we say we'll meet up with you at the Fire Battalion Chief Polk's residence at say, half past one?"

There we parted ways. Once inside the cab and heading back to Baker Street I asked Holmes whom we were expecting for lunch.

"Eh?" he said, as if not understanding.

"That special visitor you mentioned," said I. "Who might that be?"

"Empirical thinking," he answered. "As you well know, dear fellow, I need time to reflect and analyze the facts that we have uncovered thus far. And I shall do that best divested of Inspector Hopkins and his plodding speculations."

With that, he took out his black clay pipe, the one he most often used for his cerebral sessions, and began tapping the bowl with his forefinger.

"I say, Watson. Give me a bit of tobacco, would you? I seem to have forgotten mine in our lodging."

I removed my pouch from my coat pocket and handed it to him. After packing his bowl and lighting it, he sat back and appeared to enter a trance-like state. I knew better than to interrupt him and glanced out the open cab window.

The sun was breaking out through the clouds attempting to dry up the soggy London streets and I wondered just where this case might lead. Could it really involve this legendary Iron Crown? And was this Secret Anthology really what the murderer was after?

I looked back at Holmes and saw him surrounded by a hazy mixture of tobacco smoke and suddenly felt gratified that this morning's endeavor had apparently piqued his interest sufficiently enough to engage his inquisitive mind and keep him from the more undesirable pursuits.

After grabbing a quick lunch, provided with the customary alacrity of Mrs. Hudson, we were once again off to our next destination: the office of Fire Battalion Chief Oscar Polk. It was half past one when the brougham dropped us off at Battalion Station 27 and we happened to see Inspector Hopkins standing by the building smoking. He perked up when he saw us, tossed his cigarette into the gutter, and waved, after which he began a jaunty walk across the street to our location.

"I trust you had a good lunch," he said as he got to us.

"Quite," Holmes said.

"Your meeting went well?" Hopkins asked.

"Infinitely rewarding," Holmes said. "I take it that Chief Polk is not in?"

Hopkins once again appeared bewildered.

"Yes, but how the devil did you know that?"

"Elementary," Holmes said, turning and peering down the street. "You obviously had been waiting by the building for a solid bit of time." He pointed across the street toward the closed door.

I glanced that way as well and saw nothing out of the ordinary.

"Yes," Hopkins said. "He's not in. But how did you—"

Holmes waved at an approaching brougham cab.

"Two cigarettes," Holmes said. "One, which has been stamped upon by the door, and the other flung carelessly by the curb when you saw our approach. Since the average time for the consumption of one cigarette is a good eight minutes and thirty-two seconds, and the cigarette you tossed away was burned only halfway down, you had obviously been waiting for our arrival for approximately twelve minutes. Had Chief Polk been available at this location, which I'm sure you'd inquired, I rather think that you would have started your interview without us."

"Amazing," Hopkins said, his jaw still gaping.

I glanced over and caught sight of the smoldering cigarette that the inspector had dropped. A tiny trial of whitish smoke rose from the still-burning ash. Holmes had observed and indelibly recorded all this information in a split second as it passed. Yet such were the powers of his amazing analytical mind.

The cab slowed to a stop and the driver leaned down from his perch.

"Where to, gents?"

Holmes grabbed the door and held it open for me to get in first.

"I trust you know the whereabouts of Chief Polk's residence," he said to Hopkins.

The inspector gave the address to the driver and then entered the cab after me. Holmes started to enter, and then stopped, holding up his finger to indicate that the driver should wait a moment. I watched as my friend bounded across the street, stopped, and picked up the discarded cigarette. He reached into his pocket and removed his measuring tape, held the cigarette butt to the tape, and then dropped it onto the pavement once more. When he rejoined us, he jumped up into the cab with a zestful expression and said, "Twelve minutes and forty-seven seconds."

"Eh?" Hopkins said. "What's that?"

"The exact amount of time you waited for us," Holmes said as he settled onto the seat directly across from us.

The inspector appeared even more befuddled.

"How on earth did you figure that?" he asked.

Holmes reached into his coat pocket and removed his cigarette case and held it toward us. Neither Hopkins nor I indulged. Holmes took one for himself, replaced the case, and lit the cigarette with a match.

"Mr. Holmes," Hopkins said. "Are you going to tell me?"

The detective smiled. "It was the simplest of calculations. I merely measured the length of the remaining tobacco, took note of how fast it was burning, and extrapolated the amount of time it would have taken for the first part of the rolled cigarette to have been consumed."

"Amazing," Hopkins said.

"Quite right," Holmes said, his cheeks drawing upward into a mirthful grin as he glanced at me.

"Pay him no mind, inspector," I said. "He's only jesting. It's the great detective's idea of a joke."

Hopkins still seemed overwhelmed.

Holmes laughed and slapped the policeman's knee.

"It is well to remember," Holmes said, "that when dealing with something as tenebrous as murder, a bit of levity along the way can lighten the load."

"Mr. Holmes. Are you going to tell me?"

Hopkins pursed his lips and I could sense that he felt a bit humiliated by the detective's ruse.

We rode on in silence for the remainder of the trip, which I'm certain had been what Holmes had been hoping for. While I didn't agree with the shabby way that Holmes was treating poor Hopkins, I was, as I've previously mentioned, in a way relieved that my friend had seemingly shaken off the intellectual weariness that had so often proven a detriment to his well being.

When we exited the cab only a short distance from the stationhouse the cloud-streaked sunshine had virtually dispelled all of the unpleasant rain clouds from earlier. It was a pleasant walk to a nicely appointed house nestled among a heavily tree-shrouded lane. Hopkins knocked respectfully on the door when we arrived at Polk's domicile. There was no answer.

"Perhaps he didn't hear you," said Holmes. My companion rapped on the door several times only to find it slowly swing open under the force of his hand.

"How careless not to close his door," said I.

Holmes pushed past Hopkins and gained entrance to the front hallway."Halloo, Chief Polk. Are you here?"

As we stepped into the parlor we found no one at home. We looked around for a few seconds and then followed Holmes through the parlor and into the study. The room was in total disarray. Items were thrown about pell-mell, with the drawers pulled out of every desk and credenza. There, amongst the strewn papers, lying face down in the corner of the room was a man in a large pool of blood.

We rushed over and I immediately knelt to check the body for any signs of life.

I found none. There was no respiration or pulse, and the skin was cold to my touch.

I looked up at my two companions and shook my head.

"Can you confirm the identity?" Holmes asked Hopkins.

The inspector's visage was solemn as he nodded.

"It's Battalion Chief Polk," he said. "I'd better go alert the Yard."

"He's been dead less than two hours," I pronounced, lifting his arm and uncurling his fingers. "I would say just recently. Rigor mortis has not yet set in." I gently cupped his eyes closed and stepped back allowing the detective space to kneel down and examine the body.

First, he pointed to the left side of the dead man's head. It had been dealt a harsh and deadly blow, just like the one that had been described on

Withermew. I commented on this.

Holmes merely grunted and continued.

"There are no defensive wounds," he said. "Nor are there any signs of a struggle."

Then he carefully checked Polk's fingers and the cuffs of his shirt.

If he saw anything there, he didn't comment, and I knew better than to disturb his concentration by asking.

Holmes stood up and laid his hat and cane on a chair and began to move around the room, gingerly stepping over the blizzard of papers and broken shards of porcelain statues. He bent down occasionally to examine a piece of paper or a folder and then carefully discarded it.

"From the looks of this room," he said, "the murderer was searching for something, obviously some papers from the mess strewn about the parlor. Whatever it was, it was worth taking a man's life."

"Very similar to the last scene," I offered.

"Watson," Holmes said, pointing to the fireplace. "Look there, on the mantle.

I followed his gesture and saw it.

A metal box.

He quickly moved over to the fireplace and took the box in his hands. After carefully lifting the lid, he tilted it toward me. It was empty.

"I wonder," he said. "If this might be the box that was taken from Dr. Withermew's office the night of the fire."

"Well, it certainly fits the size and description of the one in question," I said. "Does that mean that the papers were here also?"

Holmes placed the box back on the mantle.

"Perhaps Polk picked it up from the Temple for some reason when he was surveying the scene after the fire had been extinguished." the detective said. "That would mean that neither of our thieves had the metal box or its contents, but rather Polk took it, being the first one in the office when the fire was out." He glanced about the room once again. "I suggest we search the room and see if we can find any papers with writing in Latin."

Holmes squatted down and started with the papers on the floor in front of the fireplace.

"The chief is a man who is very fond of letters," my companion said, holding one sheet close to his eyes. "He has written dozens of letters he had yet to post. He even wrote notes to himself. Who would need to do that, Watson?"

"Yes, who would need to do that indeed, Holmes," I said with a wry smile. "But you must admit, he does have exceptional penmanship. His cursive is outstanding."

Holmes then sat down cross legged on the floor to be nearer the heap of papers strewn about. He sorted through the detritus quickly and I could only assume that my friend had developed some sort of systematic approach for determining which pieces of paper he had picked up from the carpet were of interest, and which pieces needed only to be discarded back to the floor.

"The killer was obviously thorough," he said. "He also apparently felt he had plenty of time to go through everything in the study, judging by the fact that it all seems to have been touched and inspected. Nothing has been left unexamined."

The shrill sound of a police whistle cut through the afternoon air like a jagged knife. The police would be arriving momentarily, and who knew what they'd direct us to do. I decided to make myself useful and examine the rest of the house. I moved into the kitchen and two first floor bedrooms finding all of the drawers of every bureau and kitchen cabinet opened and rifled through. I rejoined my companion in the study and forwarded this observation.

"Thank you, old chum," he said, not bothering to look up from his sorting task.

Once more, I began looking at the scattered pieces of paper lying about for some clue as to what could have caused someone to brutally bash in the head of the Battalion Chief.

Holmes got up and moved around the study and then began to slowly go through everything that was on the desk and in the drawers.

"It is also obvious that the thief did not find what he was looking for," he said, "as there is no discernible stopping point where the search ended or an area that is untouched, signifying that the search had ended. The entire room was rifled, not an inch left unturned. Therefore, his search must have turned up nothing unless the very last piece of paper was the one for which he was searching."

Holmes continued his search and I stood waiting at the door of the study when Hopkins returned.

"Several constables are on their way," he said. "What are we looking for?"

"Please have them just guard the front door when they arrive and don't let anyone in here until I am quite finished, Inspector," said Holmes who picked up a folder and opened it on the desk.

"Now see here, Mr. Holmes," Hopkins said, obviously taking umbrage at my friend's rather blunt instructions. "I do believe that this is a matter for Scotland Yard, sir."

Without looking directly at him, Holmes spoke with a voice of authority. "Most assuredly. Now, if you don't mind, Inspector, I'd like to continue my search for the Masonic papers by myself with Watson's help for the present. I will share with you the fruits of my labor for your report." Even though he was at a positional disadvantage, his words seemed to pepper Hopkins like a round of birdshot. He slunk backward and went to the front door.

"Here, Watson, is the report on the Monday night Temple fire." He spun it around toward me.

I took the folder in my hands and sat down behind the desk and began to read. As Hopkins had said earlier, Chief Polk's notes were copious and complete, leaving out no detail. Times were marked along with the disposition of every one of his men.

"Here, Holmes," I said, and then read aloud, "he says that he suspects that the fire was started in the doorway by the two candelabra on the library side of the door after having been knocked over in a struggle suggested by the position of the body found on the scene."

"His conjectures seem plausible," Holmes said.

I scanned the report further. "He goes on to say that he had occasion to examine the body before the police took charge of it. Noticed that it was a crushing blow to the left side of the head that was probably the cause of death, and there were no signs of a struggle."

"Yes," Holmes added. "Assuming that the killer was right handed, then Withermew faced his attacker, was struck, and then fell onto his back." He paused and raised a querulous eyebrow in my direction. "And what else might we infer from this supposition?"

My mind raced, trying to keep up with his, which I knew was futile.

"No signs of a struggle," I muttered. "Could that mean that Withermew was taken by surprise?"

"Possibly," Holmes said, the hint of mirth curling the ends of his mouth slightly. "But what other avenue might it suggest?"

I compressed my lips, thinking, but could come up with nothing.

"Think, Watson, think." Holmes raised his arm in an expansive gesture. "Remember, the victim was in a room as large as this one. Could he have been surprised so thoroughly?"

The answer he was seeking still eluded me. I grabbed at what I thought might have been a plausible explanation. "Could have perhaps been dozing?"

"On his feet?" Holmes snorted something akin to a laugh. "Come, come, old boy. You can do better than that."

"Perhaps," I said slowly, still searching for some sort of conjecture that I could put forth. I swallowed and glanced up at Holmes, and then it came to me.

"He knew his attacker," I said.

Holmes smiled. "Outstanding, old boy. You've done it again."

Despite his praise, I knew that he'd dragged the answer from me through his own deductive manipulations.

The detective picked through a messy pile of papers on the desk, tossing them on the floor on top of the ones that he had already scanned. When he got to the bottom of the mess he stopped.

"Hallow," he said. "What do we have here on his desk pad?"

He pulled out a postal receipt and held it up. Holmes reached inside his jacket pocket and pulled out his magnifying lens. Holding the circular glass in front of the receipt, he studied it. "It's dated Tuesday, the 18th, Watson."

"Why, that's today," I said.

"Precisely. And it is marked at quarter past ten. That means it was posted one hour and fifteen minutes before his death."

"One hour and fifteen minutes? How can you be so exact, Holmes?" Hopkins said.

"Elementary." He lowered the magnifier. "Your pronouncement of time of death was absolutely on the mark. Polk was murdered around half past eleven, only two and one half hours ago." Holmes pointed to the large clock on the mantle. "You'll note that the timepiece is stopped at that exact time. It hasn't moved since we came into the room."

My eyes shot to the clock and I realized Holmes was right. The hands hadn't moved, and it made no ticking sound.

"I assume," he said, "that upon examination we will find that the back was tampered with in the search for whatever papers the murderer was after. Hiding papers in the back of a clock and stopping its mechanism is hardly a brilliant hiding place."

We walked over to the clock to inspect it when we heard a knock on the door. Turning, we saw that Hopkins had returned.

"The police wagon has arrived. I must take control of the crime scene, Mr. Holmes."

"By all means," Holmes said. "Why don't you let them start in that corner with the body. Please let me have a few more minutes with this room, if you could, Inspector?"

"I'm certain I can arrange that." He strode over to speak to the uniformed officers who had just come in.

"Thank you, Hopkins." Holmes held up the receipt to the light. He had taken out his magnifier and was peering at the scribbled words. "Now, if only the postal carrier had the semblance of a decent scrawl I might be able to make out this address. And the name it was sent to … It looks like the word 'Butcher.'"

"Perhaps it's a butcher shop?" I offered.

A visible frown crossed the detective's face. "I would doubt that. I would have expected better of you, my good fellow."

"Well," I said, a bit miffed by his effrontery.

Holmes continued to stare at the receipt.

"If it's the name 'Butcher,' that would leave us with at least a score of possibilities in London proper."

"What do you think it was he sent, Holmes?"

"We've got about ten minutes to try and determine that, Watson." He glanced at the flood of policemen scurrying about on the other side of the room by the body. "Hopkins will have to secure the rest of the scene for his own investigation to begin. And although I approve of his adopting some of my methods, there is always the possibility that crucial evidence may be lost. Think, man, where else could important papers be hidden?"

The detective turned around and scanned the bookcases behind the desk. There were seven shelves where books once stood. Some volumes lay on their sides, some still stacked on each other, open, and most discarded on the floor. The other shelves were taken up with old photographs of groups of firemen posing stiffly, three small sail boats, the chief on horseback with a posse of riders, a lake scene with a bunch of fishermen waving with mountains in the background, and a new pumper engine with its crew. Holmes bent down and began opening the books on the floor and shaking them upside down to see what fell out of them and then replacing them haphazardly on the shelves. The books he currently had in his hands were thick tomes of Greek philosophy, several bibles, and religious treaties. The last three books caught his attention.

After reading the titles and flipping through them, he stacked them on the corner of the desk. I noticed the titles: *Morals and Dogma*, *The Science of Spirits*, and *Deus Lo Vult*.

Weighty tomes in size and subject matter, I thought.

He stood in the center of the room as Inspector Hopkins moved in with his notebook in hand and started scribbling. The coroner finished taking his photographs of the body and they began the process of removing Chief Polk. Holmes raised his index finger to his lips and slowly rotated to take in the whole scene. Suddenly he stopped, focused on the door and the parade of Yarders coming and going.

"Stop," he yelled. "Inspector, would you kindly have your men step away from the door."

Hopkins looked startled. After a moment of silence, he waved his hands at them. The men complied, clearing themselves from the doorway.

Holmes moved across the room with the deliberate steps of the Royal Guardsmen at Buckingham Palace. He bent down at the door and picked up one of the firemen's long boots standing at attention on the mat. He thrust his arm way down into the boot, rummaged around slightly, and withdrew a handful of papers.

"Ah ha," he shouted triumphantly grabbing the second boot in the other hand and carrying it over to the desk. Soon he had emptied both boots of their contents and the desk was now filled with folded sheets of paper. "Behold, Watson, hidden papers. Now let's see if they are worth killing for."

He sat down in the chair and gathered up the pages with myself and Hopkins hovering over each shoulder like students trying to check their final grades.

"Holmes, how did you deduce that the papers were over there?" I asked.

"Yes, Mr. Holmes," Hopkins added. "I was wondering that myself."

Holmes seemed amused by our bewilderment.

"Of course you both noticed that all of the pictures on the wall were moved," he said. "This was done, no doubt, to check to see if Polk had a wall safe. Since all the pictures were replaced, and you had checked the other rooms, this meant there was no safe. Otherwise, the killer would no doubt have replaced the pictures to avoid leaving a trail. So the Battalion Chief had to have a secret place to which he trusted his most prized possessions." He walked over to the desk and cast a glance at the wide top. "With all his letter writing, I assumed that Polk was a literal man and that crochet sign in the front hallway that reads: *Roaring flames and blackened soot - I value most my trusty boots.* Spoken like a true fireman."

Holmes placed the papers onto the desk and spread them out. Both Hopkins and I walked over to view them, and I must say that neither he nor I was prepared for what we saw next. The papers were yellowed parchment and the writing was in some foreign tongue.

Not being a student of etymology, the writing was Greek to me.

"Is that French or Italian?" I asked.

"Neither," Holmes said, once again staring through his magnifying glass. "It's Latin."

CHAPTER 5
SECRETUA LIBER

"It's written completely in Latin," Holmes said as he spread the folded pages out between his bony fingers and began reading. After a few moments I saw his eyebrow form an arch. "Good Lord, Watson, do you know what we have here?"

"Haven't the foggiest," I answered, which was the truth.

"I believe that these are those missing papers that the Masons are looking for," he said. "For all their searching, we have them right here."

"Holmes, are you sure?" I asked.

"Is this what Merriweather was so secretive about?" Hopkins asked anxiously. "Pages of Latin? What do they say?"

"I'm fairly certain these are the missing Latin papers that were taken from Dr. Withermew's office," Holmes said, not revealing the substance of the papers or their purpose. "I can translate enough to know that they are in code, as Merriweather explained to us."

"Latin?" the inspector tilted his bowler back and scratched his forehead. "Who would want to steal and kill for some papers in Latin?"

"Perhaps if we can get an idea what they contain," the detective said, "we might find out."

Holmes then paused, drawing his face close to the parchment sheets and studying the edges of the papers.

"Watson, there are ink stains on a few of these sheets. And a semi-circle of ink on the bottom corner of one page."

I looked down and confirmed his observation. I detected a rush of impatience on the part of Holmes. He obviously was way ahead of both Hopkins and me.

"And there were ink stains on the cuffs of Polk's shirt," Holmes said. "I know that besides being a fairly well-off bachelor with a passion for the outdoors, a gregarious man who enjoyed outings with groups, and an intellectual, he was also a meticulous dresser. I doubt that he would lounge around with ink stains on his shirt. That means the ink stains were made before ten this morning before he posted his letters and before his murder."

I didn't have to ask Holmes how he knew those things because I had grown accustomed to my friend's extraordinary ability to take in everything as a matter of course, and then assemble the details to point to significant conjectures. Hopkins, however, was still in a state of amazement.

"I must say, Mr. Holmes," he said. "Your powers of observation and the deductions you draw are nothing short of amazing."

Holmes smiled slightly and said, "Thank you, Inspector, but we needn't take the time to belabor the obvious."

I'd figured out on my own that the ink stains on the seemingly fastidious man's cuff had had something to do with Polk's demise. I also wondered about the photos on the bookshelf as well as the titles of the books. I stared down at the stains on the documents.

Holmes reached to the far right corner of the desk and grabbed the ink bottle and brought it down to the paper. He then smoothed out the sheet and carefully placed the bottle on the corner of the page. It was a perfect fit to the semi-circle of the stain. Nodding, he quickly rifled through the other pages, stopping at each one after a thorough examination. All the rest of them he placed in a pile to his right. That left only one page in front of him.

"There you have it," he said.

Hopkins moved a step closer. "Have what, Mr. Holmes?"

Holmes raised an eyebrow in disapproval. He didn't like having to take the time to explain his cognitive machinations, but in this case, since he knew we were here only by the inspector's largess, he relented and elucidated.

"In his haste to make copies of these documents," he said. "Polk inadvertently left droplets of ink on this original sheet as he drew his pen over the pages." He pointed at the aberrant stain. "Apparently, he only copied this page. The impression of the bottom of the bottle on this particular sheet perfectly matches the circular ink stain on the paper. He also was in such a hurry to make this copy that he transferred ink from the jar to his cuff. He then folded the originals up, since there are twenty pages here, and deposited them in his boots for safe keeping. That means he sent the copied page out by post."

"Why only one page, Holmes?" I asked.

Holmes reflected on this for a moment, then said, "One can only assume that he somehow knew which page pertained to the item in question."

"But I thought you said that it was written in Latin?" Hopkins said.

"Indeed," Holmes said. "It's apparent that Polk had a working knowledge of the language, judging by the number of Latin texts he has on his bookshelves. If that is so, then someone else now has a copy of the important page of the Anthology."

Hopkins was busy writing as fast as he could in his note book. "What Anthology is that?"

Holmes and I exchanged a furtive glance.

"Just something I've taken to calling a collection of papers of which I've grown fond," he said. "Nothing for you to take particular notice of at this time, Inspector."

Hopkins nodded as he continued his furious scribbling.

"Is it possible," Holmes said, "that I might take these sheets of paper back to Baker Street with me for further examination?"

Hopkins stopped writing and looked up at him. The inspector's lips were drawn together like a miser's purse.

"It would be most irregular," he said.

"Let me give you my personal assurance," Holmes said, clapping the policeman's shoulder in a gesture of camaraderie. "That I shall personally deliver them to you for evidence inventory collection the first thing tomorrow morning?"

The police inspector seemed to vacillate slightly.

"I would," Holmes said, giving the other man's shoulder a friendly squeeze, "consider it a great personal favor."

With that Hopkins's expression brightened. "Well, Mr. Holmes, as I said, it is quite irregular, but considering how much help you've already been on this case, I don't see the harm in it. I'll wait until tomorrow to place the papers in evidence."

"Ah," Holmes said, repeating the clapping gesture. "Capital."

I retrieved a large folder from one of the desk drawers and Holmes quickly tucked the papers safely away. He picked up his hat and cane from the chair and nodded to Hopkins.

"Inspector, it has been a pleasure working with you once again. Please keep me informed of any further development in this case, as I will do the same. I would assume that the Masons will appreciate getting these papers back as soon as possible. A few days delay shouldn't matter if they know they are safe at Scotland Yard."

"Quite right," Hopkins said. "That will take a lot off of Mr. Merriweather's mind."

"And to say nothing of how good that will reflect on your ability," Holmes smiled.

With that we left Polk's house and the congestion that was caused by the throng of people gathering outside by the police wagon and the coroner's wagon. We secured a coach and started back to Baker Street.

"Spreading the butter on the biscuit with a trifle bit of thickness," I said. "Weren't you?"

Holmes laughed. "Good old Watson. Able to see through my devious subterfuges, as always."

"The mystery grows deeper, Holmes," I said. "Why would Chief Polk have the original Anthology in his possession? He must have knowingly taken it from Withermew's office. But how did he even know of its existence?"

"How indeed," Holmes said, the trace of a smile decorating his lips.

His apparent amusement intensified my determination. "Unless he is an accomplice of this Tobias, or the other unidentified, hooded fellow. If so, that makes him an accessory to murder."

The detective's smile widened.

"All good suppositions, Watson. But why would he make a copy of the important part of the Anthology that might pertain to the Iron Crown and send it to someone? And why did one of his partners come back to take him out of the equation?"

His queries caused me to fluster. I was at a point of total confusion.

"Well, whatever," I said. "But what in heaven and earth makes this blasted Anthology so valuable that it is worth the price of two men's murders?"

Holmes reached over and placed a hand upon my shoulder. "Truly, there is much we must decipher before we can bring these blackguards to justice." He leaned back into the seat and raised a finger to his chin. "Now, let us examine more of the facts before we go off on any more wild speculation. First we find out what these twenty pages of Latin have to say."

"And just how do you suggest we do that?" I asked. "Find a Latin scholar at the university to help us."

Holmes smiled. "I'm afraid that would not be propitious, dear fellow. We could hardly expose some unsuspecting scholar to the danger." He reached over and patted my arm. "Besides, I'm certain that a man of your education and learning will be more than up to the task."

"What? Why, I haven't studied Latin since ... Why I can't even remember when."

"All the better to get reacquainted as quickly as possible then."

By now the sun had completely conquered the late afternoon sky and a warm, muggy blanket of air had descended on London. I heaved out a heavy sigh.

"I almost miss the rain, Holmes. It was perfect weather to match my mood."

"Never fear, dear Watson. As I said, we have something to occupy your time when we arrive home."

He smiled again.

CHAPTER 6
THE FATE OF TOBIAS

It was almost half past eight on Wednesday morning when I happened to hear Mrs. Hudson's footfalls ascending the stairwell to our quarters. I was still wringing my wrist, trying to get the cramp out from last evening's task of copying all twenty pages of the Secret Anthology in Latin. I had forgotten why I disliked Latin so much from my university days, and finally just gave up trying to translate the long dead language that was totally beyond my comprehension. Instead, I set about transcribing the letters as accurately as I could. Holmes sat in his chair by the window smoking his black clay pipe. The upper portion of his body was engulfed in a discernible cloud of grayish smoke. I wondered what intricacies of this perplexing case he was now cogitating upon.

Our landlady's knock brought me out of my reverie.

"Come in, Mrs. Hudson," I said.

She entered with her tray of coffee, biscuits, applesauce and eggs and to make an announcement.

"Inspector Lestrade is here to see you, gentlemen."

"Thank you, Mrs. Hudson," Holmes said, rising. "You are always the bearer of pertinent news."

She cast a reproachful glance as she dropped the tray rather loudly in front of him, commenting that he had better eat all of his applesauce.

"Most assuredly," he answered, then added with a bit of a twinkle in his eye, "But don't you think the apples would have fared better had they been left to rot on the tree for a trifle bit longer?"

She simply huffed. Once back on the landing she called for the Inspector to come up.

We both listened and heard the heavy trudging upon the seventeen steps.

Moments later, the redoubtable figure of Inspector Lestrade appeared in the doorway.

"Ah," Holmes said. "Inspector Lestrade, to what do we owe this early morning visit?"

Lestrade glanced at Mrs. Hudson, who was still in earshot, and said nothing. He stepped inside and closed the door behind him.

The inspector's taciturn posture seemed to amuse Holmes. "If we had known you were coming we could have saved the price of a post as I just sent a packet of papers to Scotland Yard for Inspector Hopkins."

"Hopkins, what does he want?"

"Just a trifling matter of returning top secret missing Mason papers," Holmes chided.

Lestrade, looking more annoyed than usual, took a seat on the sofa across from Holmes and myself as we uncovered our breakfast.

"Top secret Mason papers. Masons. Another one of those special societies," he grumbled. "I wouldn't come and ask for your help if it was a situation that I could easily handle by myself, but I have hit the proverbial brick end on this one and you seem to be the best person to help me proceed."

"Certainly, Lestrade, I am always willing to lend what little talent I possess to aid Scotland Yard in pursuit of their duties. Tell me what has you in this quandary?"

"Early this morning I get called out on a dead body being reported behind the Templar's building on Westphall Way."

"Do tell." Holmes leaned back and pushed his applesauce to the far corner of his plate and cocked his head back. It was almost as if he was actually interested in what the Inspector was going to say. "And?"

"The man was found in the alley behind the building with his skull bashed in," Lestrade continued.

"How unfortunate," Holmes said.

"His name was Randall Tobias."

Holmes immediately sprang forward in his chair. "Randall Tobias, did you say? Are you absolutely sure?"

"Well, that's what a paper in his wallet said."

"Thick, curly brown hair. Mutton chops?"

"Yes." Lestrade's face tightened. "And exactly how would you know that?" There was astonishment in his voice.

"I'll explain in a moment," Holmes said. "Do go on."

Lestrade shrugged. "Well, it wasn't a robbery. We know this because his wallet was untouched. And, there was no sign of a struggle."

"You seem to be getting a lot of that lately," Holmes said.

"I beg your pardon?"

The detective waved his hand dismissively and Lestrade continued.

"When I asked to speak to the man in charge in the Templar's building, I had to wait over twenty minutes until this big, snooty fellow comes out and says he's..." the Inspector quickly consulted his notebook, "a Frenchman called Duke Jean Pierre Bouchard. Says he's the Grand Master of the Knights Templars." He paused again and cast an inquisitive look at Holmes. "You ever heard of them buggers?"

"Indeed I have," Holmes replied. "I seem to be meeting a whole lot of Grand Masters lately as well."

Lestrade sniffed and went on. "Well, the minute I start asking him questions, he goes and claims that he has some sort of diplomatic immunity. I got nowhere with him. Holmes. I just don't speak their language. He was evading all of my questions. Wouldn't let his assistant answer any questions either. He acted so high and mighty, like he's so far above me." Lestrade snorted in apparent disgust, then bunched up his lips.

Holmes seemed to be enjoying the other man's obvious angst.

"So what may I do for you, Inspector?" he asked.

It took Lestrade several seconds to answer, and when he did, he kept his eyes on the floor between them. "I was thinking, that perhaps with your reputation, you might consider talking with them. Maybe can get some answers? You speak their language."

Holmes raised an eyebrow and smiled. "This case does hold some interest for me, Lestrade. I'll be happy to accompany you back to the site of this murder. Of course, I assume that you've already removed the body from the scene?"

"Yes. I know you don't like that. But the Duke was quite insistent. He had some heavy connections at the Yard."

"That seems to be prevalent, too," Holmes mused.

"I can tell you that there wasn't much blood at the scene, so I'm sure that he wasn't killed there. His body must have been put there after he was murdered."

"Of course," my companion said. "Well, we know the victim and the circumstances, so that will have to suffice. Come, Watson, take your biscuits with you and do take another sip of tea and let's be off. I'll gladly leave this applesauce for Eve to play with in her Garden of Eden. Let's go to the aid of the good Inspector."

Once outside and in a brougham, we settled in for the trip to Westphall Way. I could see the tiny fires burning behind my friend's eyes.

After a time he spoke, "Inspector, what do you know of the Templars?"

"Not much, I must confess." He leaned forward. "What about you?"

"I've come across them in my research for my monogram about old English charters," Holmes answered. "Their history goes way back to 1100 A.D., I believe. They were a military order of knights founded to protect travelers and caravans bound for the Holy Land, answerable only to the pope himself. They called themselves the Sacred Order of Solomon's Temple, which was shortened to the Knights Templar over time. They took vows of poverty, chastity, didn't curse, drink, or smoke."

"Sounds like a sorry lot if you ask me," Lestrade said.

"They must have had a difficult time maintaining their lineage," I said. "Considering the chastity vow."

Holmes chuckled. "Why, Watson, I was just thinking that, except for that aspect, you might have made a good Templar."

I made it a point not to reply to such an outrageous bit of tomfoolery.

My companion reached inside his coat and pulled out his cigarette case, opened it, extracted a cigarette and searched for a match.

"Their services," he continued, "were invaluable during the Crusades where they acquired many estates and set up preceptories along the routes to Jerusalem. They acquired extensive land holdings in England and France along with starting a network of banks to protect the money and goods of travelers. Deposit your money here in England with the Templars and withdraw the same amount when you arrive in the Holy Land. Quite ingenious at the time." He patted his pockets some more. "The Templars also came into possession of a good many holy relics from their participation in the Crusades. These priceless relics were brought back to England, France and Italy…Eventually, they were hidden away in various locations. The Templars became very rich and influential in no time at all."

"So much for abiding by that vow of poverty," said I.

"Very true. But it only lasted until the early 1300's when King Edward II, who was jealous of the Templars' power and wealth, confiscated most of their extensive land holdings and gave the rest to the Order of the Hospital of St. John, a rival order of knights. After that the Templars gradually faded into history."

"So much for abiding by the vow of poverty."

Holmes continued to search his pockets for a box of matches. Seeing his distress, Lestrade pulled out a match, struck it on the coach door, and held it toward him.

Holmes placed the cigarette between his lips and leaned forward so that the tip was engulfed by the flame.

"Thank you, Inspector." He exhaled some smoke. "Now where was I? Oh yes, in the 18th century the Freemasons came into being with the consolidation of the guilds and adopted the old Templar traditions, symbols, rituals, hierarchy, and anything else they could think of, including the creation of Grand Masters. But as you can see, the Knights Templars made a comeback of sorts and are still around."

"So," said Lestrade, "that's where this uppity 'Boot-shard' comes in," mangling the Frenchman's name on purpose.

"Boot-shard," I laughed.

"Good grief, Watson, that's it. You've done it again."

"I have?" I couldn't help but feel a bit pleased. "Do you mind telling me what I've done?"

"The scribbled name by the postal carrier," Holmes said. "'Butcher.' It no doubt alludes to the French pronunciation, 'Bouchard.' The post from Polk was sent to this Bouchard, who's a Templar. I should have seen it before. The books on his shelf; *Morals and Dogma* by Pike, *Science of the Spirits* by Levi ... Both are books by Masons. And *Deus lo Vult*—a Templar book. Polk was both a Mason and a Templar." Holmes blew a thin column of smoke from his lips. "The copy of the coded page of the Secret Anthology was sent to the Templars."

"What page of what secret?" Lestrade asked, as confused as a blind man on a crowded street.

"Oh, nothing to concern yourself about, Inspector" Holmes said. "Just a little conundrum that the good doctor and I are working on."

"Which just got a little more convoluted," I said.

My friend smiled. "Yes, there are a few more questions of my own that I would like to ask your Duke Bouchard."

After a short time we pulled up to a stately brownstone building where several steps led up to two well varnished walnut doors. Inspector Lestrade did the honors and secured us entrance to an opulent foyer with hand carved mahogany walls and bronze gilded chairs. The floor was a classic black and white checkerboard pattern.

"It appears that these Templars here must have forgotten to take that vow of poverty as well," said I.

We were greeted by a butler who ushered us into a sumptuous parlor decorated with several Queen Ann chairs gathered around the large fireplace which dominated the room.

"Won't you gentlemen come in and be seated?" the butler said. "The Duke will be down to see you shortly." He directed us towards the chairs and then made his discreet exit.

"I wonder how long we'll have to wait for his high and mighty Dukeness to appear," Lestrade said with venom in his voice.

Over the fireplace, a painting depicting several men who seemed to stare out at us from the dark blue and black hues. I was most certain it was the work of a Dutch Master, although for the life of me I couldn't recall which one. Holmes paced the room, taking in everything he could, sizing up the surroundings. I had little doubt he was looking forward to doing the same regarding the occupant he would soon meet.

Into the parlor stepped a rather tall man with dark brown eyes framed by bushy salt and pepper eyebrows. He had a full head of wavy hair and beard to match. His strong chin gave him a regal appearance. He was accompanied by a shorter man with thinning brown hair and a set of droopy eyes.

"I am Duke Jean Pierre Bouchard," the tall man said, looking us up and down. His gaze settled on Lestrade and he frowned. "And you are the policeman who wasted my time earlier. Bringing two more of your confederates back with you does not impress me in the least."

Holmes immediately stepped forward and offered his hand to the Duke. "May I take this moment to introduce myself? I'm Sherlock Holmes, consulting detective to Scotland Yard. And this is my associate, Dr. John H. Watson, MD. It is a pleasure to make your acquaintance, Duke Bouchard."

Reluctantly the Duke reached out and shook my companion's hand.

"Again, I have nothing to say to you." His frown deepened. "As I told this one before—" His fingers fluttered dismissively in Lestrade's direction. "I have diplomatic immunity, as I am a French council and Grand Master of the Templars here in England."

"You may be the Grand Master," said Holmes," but you can claim no diplomatic immunity as this is not an embassy and you are not an ambassador. So, if you would be so kind as to answer a few of our questions, we shall then be on our way."

There was a deathly silence in the room as if Hades, the Greek god of death, had himself passed through the parlor. The Frenchman's lips pursed and then stretched into a frown. "Very well, Mr. Holmes, I shall answer your few questions."

"Excellent. We are here to inquire about a man found dead in the alley behind your building this morning."

"Bah," the Duke said. "I know nothing of this."

Holmes seemed unperturbed by the denial. "The man's name was Randall Tobias."

"*Du rein*," the Duke said. "Nothing."

"Are you certain you have never met the man before?"

The Duke pursed his lips once more, then shook his head.

"Interesting," Holmes said. "Do you have any idea why he would be here?"

"No, I do not know this ridiculous man or why he should be here."

"So, he did not come here to see you or anyone here that you know of?"

"No, of course not. We do not allow anyone off the streets to come in here." He took the moment to cast a disparaging glance at each one of us before adding. "Are we now *fini*?"

"Not quite yet." Holmes placed his forefinger to his lips. "May I ask who found the body?"

The Duke heaved a sigh, and then gestured to the man standing off to the left. "Mr. Hager here."

Holmes canted his head and looked at the other man. "Mr. Hager, when did you find the body of Mr. Tobias?"

"Must've been about eight-thirty, to the best of my recollection." As if he was seeking permission to speak, Hager stole a quick, furtive glance at the Duke. "But he wasn't dead yet. He was moaning and bleeding a plenty. By the time I got back to him with some help from inside he had passed away."

"Interesting." Holmes stroked his chin. "Can you tell me the condition of the man when you found him?"

"His condition?"

"Yes," Holmes said. "His condition. Were his clothes torn? Did it look as if he'd been attacked? Were there any bruises that you could see on his hands or face?"

Hager glanced over to Bouchard, who nodded. The shorter man's words then dribbled out with rapidity. "Why, no, sir. The only thing I saw was the big gash in the side of his head. Looked like he was clubbed upon several times, real hard."

"Was there any weapon, a club or truncheon lying nearby?"

"No, sir," he replied. "Not that I could see."

Holmes made a point of staring intently at the shorter man. For a moment I wondered if he would wilt like a flower. "Thank you, Mr. Hager. You've been extremely helpful."

"Are we now quite done here?" Bouchard asked impatiently.

"I only have one more question," Holmes said. "And it's for you, Duke." He waited a beat, and then asked, "Did you receive a letter in the post on last Tuesday?"

The Frenchman's brow wrinkled.

"A letter? What kind of question is this?" He seemed to be on the verge of sputtering. "Why—I do not remember on which days I received letters. This is absurd."

Holmes persisted. "It's a simple question. Did you receive a letter by messenger on Tuesday last?"

Once again the Duke's mouth tightened. "No, I did not. And, furthermore, I will waste no more time on this...this...preposterous intrusion. I am finished here." He abruptly turned and marched out of the room.

"And so are we," Holmes announced. "Thank you for your time, Mr. Hager. As I said, you've been most helpful. Come, Inspector, we've gotten what we came for. Good day."

There was a bewildered look on Lestrade's face as we followed Hager to the door. As we reached the entrance, Hager glanced about quickly and then put his hand on Holmes' arm.

"Sir, you didn't ask me this, but it might be important to the police." His voice was a low whisper. "The man said something to me before I went in for help."

"Good Lord, man that could be of the utmost importance," Holmes said. "Tell me exactly what he said."

"Well, he only muttered a few words." Hager looked around again, then leaned forward. He said, 'Pastor Thaddeus, forgive me.' That was it. Just those few words. I don't know any Pastor Thaddeus. Do you, sir?"

"No, but I intend to before the day is out. Mr. Hager, you've been most helpful to the police. Inspector Lestrade here will remember your cooperation in this case. Thank you, again."

Holmes shook the man's hand and he left the brownstone with a spring in his step.

While Lestrade flagged down a cab, I turned to my companion," So what do you make of it all, Holmes?"

"Another mystery, inside a riddle, wrapped up in a conundrum," Holmes said.

"That's putting it mildly," I answered.

"What I need to know," he said, "is who killed Tobias and why? Also, for what did he need to be forgiven?"

"A mystery, inside a riddle, wrapped up in a conundrum." I smiled. "I rather like that. Catchy little phrase. Perhaps I'll use it someday in one of my writings."

"A catchy phrase indeed," he said. "But let's make sure we can properly unravel it first."

The four-wheeler pulled up and we all got in. Lestrade seemed ready to burst, waiting to ask his questions. We gave the coachman the destination and as soon as he slid the door shut, Lestrade bent forward, his elbows pressed upon his knees.

"Well," he said, settling into his seat. "What did it all mean, Holmes?"

"Inspector, it is both puzzling and illuminating at the same time."

Lestrade snorted. "You're telling me what I already know."

The trace of a slight smile graced the detective's lips.

"Interestingly enough," Holmes began, "we happen to be working on an investigation that parallels this one in that involves the victim in this case."

"What?" Lestrade's face bore a look of total confusion.

Holmes stroked his chin before continuing. "We were actually hoping to track down this Tobias fellow to question him about the fire that occurred Monday night at the Masonic Lodge and the murder of one, Dr. Withermew. Questioning is now, obviously, out of the question."

"The murder of whom?" Lestrade asked incredulously. "Are you trying to tell me that this murder victim here might possibly be a murder suspect himself?"

"Quite possibly," Holmes said. "And why would he be at the house of the Templars when he has no apparent connection to them?"

Lestrade's lower lips protruded. He said nothing.

"Let's take stock of what we do know," Holmes said. "We know that three men, Withermew, Polk and Tobias, all share a commonality in these two investigations. In all probability, they may very well killed by the same man."

"What makes you think that?" Lestrade asked.

"The violent methodology in each instance," Holmes said. "Each was perpetrated by someone with a predilection to violent behavior, and this individual was probably known to all three victims."

"Why would you think that?" Lestrade asked.

"That shall remain a mere conjecture on my part for the time being, until I can confirm my suspicions," Holmes said. "But concentrating on what we do know, it's safe to assume that Polk sent a copy of some stolen papers to Bouchard on Tuesday."

"Why would he do that?" Lestrade asked.

I must admit, I had the same question.

"The answer is obvious," Holmes said. "The dearly departed Mr. Polk was a Mason, but he was also affiliated with the Templars. Or at least wanted them to have a copy of the riddle."

"And," I added. "Bouchard lied about getting them, did he not?"

"Most assuredly," Holmes said. "Did you notice his visible awkwardness when confronted by the question, Watson?"

"I most certainly did." I felt proud of myself for having kept up, at least for the moment, with my friend's amazing deductive prowess.

"Why would he lie about it?" Lestrade asked.

"I'm sure that Inspector Hopkins hasn't had time to receive the envelope containing the papers that I sent him earlier this morning," Holmes said. "That means that both the Masons and the Templars will have the coded pages detailing the location of the item which they seek."

"Coded pages?" Lestrade seemed more baffled than ever.

"The Anthology," Holmes said.

I made a mental note that Holmes had conveniently left us out of the list of those who had copies of those same coded pages.

"Holmes, what in blazes are you going on about?" Lestrade blurted out. "Coded pages? Location of what item? And what does Hopkins have to do with it?" The Inspector appeared as bewildered as a dog chasing his own tail.

"Nothing for you to be concerned about," Holmes said. "I assure you of that."

Lestrade frowned.

"I'm glad to have been of service to you, Lestrade," Holmes said. "Now, would you be so kind as to drop us off at the Masonic Lodge? I'd like to see Mr. Merriweather and break the news about Tobias and tell him of the strong probability that the Templars have a copy of his missing papers."

"I still don't know what to make of all this?" Lestrade said as his mouth twisted into a scowl. "And to think I came to you in good faith, asking for your assistance."

Holmes shifted his weight to sit closer to me, but still addressed the Inspector.

"Lestrade, may I suggest that you immediately ascertain where this fellow, Tobias, lived and then conduct a thorough search of his premises. See if you can find any clues as to why he might have been killed at one location, and then dropped off at the Templar's building. If you find anything would you be so kind as to let me know?"

"I'll be certain to do that, Holmes." The Inspector knocked on the side and when the slot opened up, he gave the directions to the driver to proceed to the Masonic Lodge. He was scratching his neck, still puzzled.

"In the meantime, Watson," Holmes whispered to me. "You and I are going to speak to Mr. Merriweather about this Pastor Thaddeus. His name has come up once too often to be ignored now."

CHAPTER 7
PASTOR THADDEUS

We bade Inspector Lestrade good day at the sprawling entrance of the Masonic Temple building. Once inside we were recognized by the large doorman who now greeted us heartily as fellow Masons and ushered us into Merriweather's office.

"I'm afraid I have some bad news for you, "Holmes began.

Merriweather's face grew concerned and he leaned forward.

"What is it?"

"Mr. Tobias," Holmes said. "He was found dead this morning on the other side of London."

"Oh my God," Merriweather exclaimed, "this is horrible. How did it happen?"

Holmes waited a beat, and then said, "He was bludgeoned to death."

The news seemed to strike Merriweather like a blow from a hammer. He staggered slightly.

"My Lord. Who could have done such a thing?" He steadied himself on the corner of his desk. "And what does this do to your investigation of Dr. Withermew's murder? Tobias was the primary suspect. Does this mean that the case will never be solved?"

"I wouldn't say that," Holmes answered. "Watson and I will still pursue the investigation until we are satisfied that we know who killed Dr. Withermew. This will just make our job little bit more difficult, I dare say."

Merriweather seemed to be regaining some of his composure.

"There was a slight complication regarding his death," Holmes said.

The other man's brow furrowed. "Complication?"

"Yes. He was found in the alley behind the Templar's building."

"What?" Merriweather exclaimed, once again looking as rattled as if he'd been smote. "Behind the Templar's. Why…this is an outrage. The Templars are responsible for the death of Tobias? They shall pay for this vile crime," he shouted.

Holmes held up a hand that seemed to quiet the man's outrage. "Mr. Merriweather, let me first say that there is no proof that the Templars were involved in any way with Tobias's death. From what little we do know, he was killed somewhere else, and his body was dumped there much later."

Merriweather was actually panting.

Holmes tried to assure him. "The only connection with the Templars at this time may just be the fact that the alley happens to be behind the Templar's building. Or perhaps not. In any case, it is far too early to jump to any such conclusions."

The veins slowly shrunk in the Grand Master's neck, his breathing returned to normal, and his face resumed its regular shade of pink. He again fell back onto the corner of his desk for support. We let a minute pass for him to regain his composure.

"The man who killed him and Dr. Withermew must be brought to justice," he said pushing himself up from the edge of the furniture. "At least I have the good fortune to thank you for recovering the Secret Anthology. I've been informed that Inspector Hopkins has it safe at Scotland Yard and will be returning it shortly to me. It's a relief knowing it will soon be safely back under our protection."

Holmes began to pace several steps back and forth before Merriweather's desk, one arm tucked behind his back.

"About that," he said, "I have some further news that complicates this issue. I'm sure that Inspector Hopkins told you that we found the Anthology in Polk's possession."

"Yes. That was good news that it was safe with a fellow Mason. It was fortuitous that Polk picked up the metal box and saved it from the ashes that night."

"Yes. Most fortuitous," Holmes said, casting a quick wink my way. He turned back to face Merriweather. "By the way, I'm sure you knew that Battalion Chief Polk, besides being a Lodge member of the Masons, was also a Templar, correct?"

"He was what?" came the incredulous reply.

"Yes," Holmes said. "He was a loyal Templar, going so far as to make a copy of the section of the Anthology that pertained to the Iron Crown, and then sent it off to the Templar Bouchard."

"This is an outrage!" the Grand Master sputtered. "Our holy document in the hands of that Templar! It is unimaginable!" His face became a crimson shade once more and he clenched his fists. His eyes narrowed with hate focused on the mention of the word Templar.

"Get hold of yourself, man," I said. "You'll give yourself an apoplectic."

"You don't understand—" he muttered.

"What good will it do them?" Holmes asked, the trace of the smile still noticeable on his lips. "I mean, if it is coded, and they cannot decipher it—"

"Because they never should have seen it," Merriweather shouted. "Perhaps they have scholars who *can* decipher it. Perhaps they have other texts of their own that will help them understand the clues. Perhaps they can figure it out and decode it and find a way to get to the Iron Crown," Merriweather said through gritted teeth. "It must never fall into their hands."

"Well," Holmes said in the calmest of tones. "Must I remind you that in the meantime, we have three unsolved murders on *our* hands. And we have a name that we would like to follow up on."

"A name?" Merriweather grunted. "What name?"

"With his dying words, Tobias mentioned a Pastor Thaddeus. I believe you identified him as a past Grand Master, correct?"

"And what would Thaddeus have to do with this?" an agitated Merriweather growled, his face flushed with anger.

"That is what we are going to find out," my companion said. "Now what can you tell us the whereabouts of this Thaddeus?"

"Why would you be interested in him?"

"Just curious. Where would I find him to ask him why his name would be on the lips of a dying man?"

Merriweather shrugged.

"Come, come," Holmes said. "Out with it."

Merriweather's frown deepened. "All right, all right. But let me warn you, the truth isn't very pretty."

"It seldom is where murder is concerned," Holmes said, giving the man a stern look.

After a few moments more, Merriweather continued. "It is as I said. Pastor Ezra Thaddeus is the past Grand Master. The one immediately preceding me."

"Yes," Holmes said. "Do go on."

"That was some time ago." Merriweather heaved a sigh. "Now he's little more than a harmless old man. Addle pated. Often appears quite mad, I'm told."

"It would be best for us to judge that on our own," Holmes said. "Where is he?"

"He's at St. Mary's. He has a private room there. He was quite successful as a pastor and had several fortunes bequeathed to him. He is well looked after."

"Then Watson and I shall pay him a visit," Holmes said, picking up his hat and his cane and moving towards the door.

Merriweather straightened up. "Wait, Mr. Holmes, what do you intend to do about the Templars having the Anthology?"

"I intend to do nothing. That is your concern. My immediate concern is the three murders that are before me. You shall have your original Anthology returned to you shortly. I believe I've done my duty here. Good day, sir."

↫

Holmes and I knew our way back to the entrance by now and we were on the street and in no time we were hailing a hansom. The sun shone down brightly on London dispelling any remnants of the past day's rain. Since it was around noon, we decided to stop off past Park Boulevard at a fine little restaurant that we both appreciated for lunch. In an hour we were on our way across the city to St. Mary's Hospital on South Wharf Road. It was a grand private hospital familiar to both Holmes and me. I had seen many a patient there during the years of my practice.

After inquiring as to where we might find Pastor Ezra Thaddeus, we were directed to the private wing of the hospital. We made our way to that area and went down the hall to his room. It was rather spacious, normally holding four beds, but now was only accommodating the single solitary bed, a four-poster covered by a stunning yellow duvet. A bright room, made even brighter by the sunlight pouring in through the parted drapes of the windows on its southern exposure. It was nicely appointed, like a small parlor, complete with a sofa, several chairs, and two small tables with a newspaper upon one of them. Pastor Thaddeus was seated in an easy chair in his cashmere robe and slippers. There, before us, was a man of average height, an oval of white hair ringed his head and swept down the back of his neck giving his angular face an even sharper appearance. His eyes were a pale blue.

"Pastor Ezra Thaddeus, I presume?" Holmes took off his hat and bowed politely.

"Yes, young man. What can I do for you?" he spoke in a raspy voice.

"My name is Sherlock Holmes and this is my associate Dr. John H. Watson. We would like to visit with you and ask you a few questions if you don't mind?"

"Oh, another doctor. I think the doctors here are such a nice bunch of fellows." He squinted as he surveyed my visage. "Pardon me, but I haven't seen you before, have I?"

"No, sir," I answered him. "I can assure that you haven't."

His features seemed to twitch a bit, and then resume a more relaxed expression. "Sometimes I have a bit of trouble remembering." He chuckled. "Do sit down, gentlemen. Here, doctor, you sit right here, closest to me." He motioned to the nicely upholstered chair to his right.

"Thank you, Pastor Thaddeus." I took the proffered seat. "May I ask how are you feeling today?"

"Just fine, sir. Just fine. My health has been fine for some time now, ever since I shook that cold I had a several weeks ago. Or was it several months ago? I'm not sure." His eyes seemed to soften and glaze over.

Suddenly, a rather tall, athletic looking man wearing a long, white coat appeared in the doorway. His deep set eyes, staring out over an aquiline nose, were fixed upon Holmes and me.

"Gentlemen, may I inquire whom might you be, and why are you in Pastor Thaddeus' room?" His tone was stern and rather accusatory.

My friend sprang to his feet and proffered his open hand to diffuse the situation.

"Mr. Sherlock Holmes at your service," he said. "And this is my esteemed colleague, Dr. John H. Watson, M.D."

The man stared at me and a reddish flush crept over his cheeks.

"You're a doctor?" he asked.

"Yes," I said. "I am."

"As, I take it, are you," Holmes said.

The man transferred his gaze back to him, and then nodded.

Holmes waited a moment and then continued.

"We are here at the behest of Mr. Merriweather to see how Pastor Thaddeus is getting along, and to ask him if he can be of any help in sorting out a matter of some importance."

The fellow regarded us for several more seconds, and then his face drew tight.

"Oh," he said. "My apologies, gentlemen. I didn't mean to be so short." His tone had softened substantially. "I'm Doctor Samuel Hester, the Pastor's primary care physician. I've grown rather fond of him, and tend to be a bit over protective."

"I assure you that our intentions are completely honorable and innocuous," Holmes said.

Dr. Hester showed us a questioning look,

"Am I right in assuming you are *the* Sherlock Holmes?" he asked. "The great detective?"

A smile graced Holmes' lips. "It seems my reputation has preceded me."

"He's one and the same," I took the opportunity to say.

Dr. Hester took a visible step back. It was as if he'd just found himself in the presence of royalty.

"It's an honor to meet you, sir," he said. "I've heard a great deal about you. And you as well, Dr. Watson."

"Thank you," I said.

"I didn't mean to be brusque," Dr. Hester said. "It's just that Pastor Thaddeus doesn't get many visitors, and I was startled by your appearance here. Of course you are welcome. Please be seated."

The detective returned to his seat and appeared to carefully study the other man's broad shoulders, rounded jaw, strong hands, and sinewy arms. I did the same, trying to surmise what had piqued my friend's interest. Dr. Hester was clean shaven and ruggedly handsome. The flush in his cheeks had subsided.

Holmes turned back to Thaddeus.

"I'm glad that you are feeling well today, Pastor," he said. "Mr. Merriweather sends his warmest regards. I was wondering if we can ask you about a man called Randall Tobias. Would you happen to know him?"

The pastor brought a hand to his mouth, then brushed at his chin. "Randall. Well, of course. What a fine fellow. One of the best men on this earth."

Suddenly Thaddeus' eyes grew sharp and focused. His voice was firm and strong. He sat slightly more upright in his chair and clasped his hands in his lap. "Why he comes several times a week to visit me. I hear his confession and we talk for hours."

I kept an eye on the pastor as the confusion that he showed upon our arrival had considerably lessened. I recognized his symptoms as early dementia; a fleeting loss of cognitive function and memory, an inability to concentrate brought on by old age. The affliction comes and goes, some bouts more serious than others. At times the patient is entirely lucid. The mention of Tobias's name seemed to trigger this short recovery.

"Well, the confession part might have something to do with it," Holmes said softly. "I have some very bad news for you, Pastor. I don't know any other way to tell this to you, so I will just come out and say it. Mr. Tobias is deceased."

"What?" the pastor's jaw gaped. "When?"

"Earlier today, I'm afraid," Holmes said.

The old man took in a series of rapid breaths. "How did this happen?"

Holmes waited a beat before saying, "Regrettably, he was murdered across town early this morning."

"Oh, God, no," Thaddeus cried. "Not Randall. Not poor, innocent Randall. Who could have done such a thing?" Tears poured from Thaddeus's eyes. He fumbled retrieving the handkerchief from his robe pocket. "Aside from his gambling habit, he was a sterling individual. Came to visit me often, you know."

So this Tobias had a propensity to gamble, I thought. Interesting.

I turned my eyes from the old man and regarded the younger one. Hester seemed much more unfazed than the pastor, who was still beside himself with grief.

The bright sunlight stood in sharp contrast to the pall that suddenly fell over the room. Everyone sat there in silence as the Pastor wept uncontrollably. Respectfully, my companion gave him time to grieve before speaking again.

"There is something I must tell you concerning the innocence of Randall Tobias," said Holmes. "Last Sunday at the fire that struck the Masonic Lodge, he was spotted running from the scene."

Thaddeus wiped at his nose. "A fire?"

"Yes," Holmes said. "And not only that. A man, a Dr. Withermew, was in the building. His office."

"Was he killed in the fire?" Dr. Hester asked.

"Actually," Holmes said, turning toward him. "He was murdered before the blaze was set."

"What makes you think that Randall had anything to do with that?" Dr. Hester asked.

"He was placed by witnesses in the vicinity of the office."

Dr. Hester said nothing.

Holmes continued. "There was also the theft of a document that was in Dr. Withermew's possession."

Hester's brow furrowed. "A document. What type of document?"

"I can only say," Holmes said, "that it concerns a certain...Anthology."

The pastor perked up at those words.

"An anthology?" he said. "Are you referring to the Secret Anthology?"

"One and the same," Holmes said, turning back to him. "I take it you're familiar with it?"

"The Secret Anthology?" the pastor said. "But of course."

"Pastor, please," Dr. Hester began. "I must advise not to get yourself into a state of over-excitement."

Thaddeus cut him off with the wave of a hand. "Please go on, Mr. Holmes."

Holmes smiled benignly and then tipped his head slightly, making a direct and very obvious glance in Dr. Hester's direction.

"Perhaps we should be more circumspect?" he said.

Thaddeus shook his head vehemently.

"You can speak freely in front of Samuel, Mr. Holmes. He is privy to all of my secrets. Not only is he my caretaker, but we are the best of friends."

Holmes nodded in acknowledgement.

I noticed a frown forming on Hester's mouth.

"But see here," Thaddeus said. "Are you saying that Randall Tobias stole the Secret Anthology?"

"It appears that may have been the way things unfolded," Holmes said.

"Balderdash!" Thaddeus said. "Entirely out of the question." He paused to wipe the tears from his eyes with the handkerchief and then began rocking gently, back and forth, in his chair.

"Randall and I are the best of friends," he said. "He comes here to visit me often. And we talk. I hear his confessions."

Holmes and I exchanged glances.

It appeared that the old man was slipping from lucidity a bit more, which is sometimes the case with such afflictions.

"It would be best to speed things up," I said, *sotto voce*.

Holmes nodded.

"That may very well be true," the detective continued, "And I'm certain his visits have had a salubrious effect on both you and him."

"I hear his confessions, you know," the old man said.

"Excellent," Holmes said. "Now, getting back to the incident I described, it seems that there was another unidentified man present that night who also might have taken the Secret Anthology. Somehow it found its way into the hands of one, Battalion Chief Oscar Polk."

"He has it?" Thaddeus asked.

"Not any longer," Holmes said. "It's now in the hands of Scotland Yard."

"Scotland Yard?" Dr. Hester said. "Has this Polk fellow been charged with the theft?"

"No," Holmes said. "At this point all of his alleged transgressions are being judged by a higher power."

"A higher power?"

"He, too, was murdered," Holmes said. He turned back to the pastor. "I have reason to believe that before Polk died he made a copy of part of the Secret Anthology."

Thaddeus perked up. "He did? What did he do with it?"

Once again, Holmes delayed his reply for several seconds before answering. "He sent it off to the Templars."

Tears continued to roll down Thaddeus' cheek.

Dr. Hester shook his head. "Please, don't over-excite yourself."

Thaddeus again shook off the warning. "I knew that Randall took the Anthology to Chief Polk. But why would Polk make a copy of it?"

"Wait," I said incredulously. "You knew that Tobias took the Anthology and gave it to Polk?"

"Yes, of course," Thaddeus declared. "We were trying to decipher it."

"Decipher it?" I said.

Thaddeus' head turned toward me and from his expression I gathered that he thought he must be addressing the village idiot. "Of course. Randall and I have spoken quite often about the Secret Anthology and the Iron Crown."

"The Iron Crown?" Holmes said, obviously trying to draw more information out of the old man by proffering ignorance.

"Yes," the old man said, his visage twisting into an expression of distain. "It is the most prized relic in all of Christendom. I have been trying to translate the Latin verses and decipher its clues for many years. I have spent many months trying to master the riddle of the code with Randall right here."

Holmes shot forward in his chair. "What? You have a copy of the Anthology in your possession?"

A chuckle escaped Thaddeus' lips, sending more teardrops running down his cheeks. "No, no, of course not. I memorized it during my earliest days as Grand Master. But then my memory began to get a little worse.

"Randall and I have spoken quite often about the Secret Anthology and the Iron Crown."

I was trying to recite it to Randall so he could work on it. We were making headway on it, too. But I was worried about its safety there in the Masonic Hall. I never thought that Withermew was the most intelligent man when it came to protecting important papers and valuables. He used to hide his toffee on a bookshelf in a glass jar. He said no one would think of looking for it there. In a glass jar."

I shook my head. The eccentricities and logic of Mason Grand Masters were mysterious things indeed. What I found more amazing was that anything at all had remained a secret within their ranks and possession.

"Pastor," the detective continued, "do you remember the last time you spoke with Randall Tobias?"

"Certainly, I speak with him all the time. He comes here to visit me, you know. I hear his confessions as well."

"No." I could tell that Holmes was struggling to maintain a gentleness in his tone. "I meant the last day that you saw him. When was that?"

"Oh." The old man stroked his chin once more. His eyes had a dreamy look to them. "That must have been ... last Monday. Or was it the Monday before that? No, two weeks ago. It was before last Christmas. Of that I'm certain. I think..." His words faded into oblivion as his voice trailed off.

"Pastor, please listen very carefully to me." Holmes pressed the subject. "Did you speak to him in the last few days?"

"Oh, in the last few days?" the old man paused to take in a few more deep breaths. "Why, yes, I'm certain I did. It was Monday. Or was it the Monday past?"

I turned to Dr. Hester who was listening intently. "Can you be of any help in this matter?"

He said nothing and slowly shook his head, his expression remaining impassive.

I persisted. "Do you recall the last time that Tobias visited Pastor Thaddeus here?"

"I'm afraid I can't help you there, old boy," Dr. Hester said. "I look in on the Pastor virtually every day just to make sure that he is getting the proper care, but I do have other responsibilities. I can't be here all day long. As to anyone else visiting him, they could have quite possibly have been here in any of the last few days and I wouldn't know about it."

"Thank you, Dr. Hester," Holmes said. "Pastor Thaddeus, do you recall what you and Tobias spoke about the last time you were together?"

"I'm not sure. I do know that I heard his confession. I always hear his confession, you know."

"Holmes," I leaned closer to my friend and spoke in a whisper. "This line of questioning is getting us nowhere. I'm afraid the Pastor is slipping back into senility. It is a symptom of his disease. We cannot put much stock in anything that he says."

"Let's hear him out, Watson. We may yet find the truth somewhere in his words." Turning back to the old man, Holmes spoke in a loud voice. "And what can you tell me about his confession?"

Thaddeus appeared shocked. "Why, I can't tell you anything spoken under the bonds of the sacrament of confession."

"Of course not. And I'm not asking you to." Holmes kept his voice smooth and soothing. "But perhaps can you tell me what you and Randall spoke of after that?"

The old man smiled. "Well, Randall told me that he took the Secret Anthology to Polk." He blinked several times, as if startled by his own words. "At least, I think he did."

He brought his finger to his lips in contemplation.

"It's very important, Pastor," Holmes said. "Can you recall exactly what was said?"

The old man pursed his lips, then a beatific smile overtook him. "Why, yes, he did tell me that he had the Anthology. I remember that now."

Suddenly, his expression grew nebulous once more. "But why would Randall have the Secret Anthology?" Thaddeus stopped and looked up to the ceiling as if the answer were floating somewhere up above. "I don't recall."

"You must recall," Holmes said, his voice rising from plaintiveness to a tone of authority. "Lives may be at stake."

"Oh, yes...yes...I do remember," the old man said. "It was to try to figure it out. He took it to decipher it. Gave it to Polk because Polk was his best friend since their school days, and well-versed in Latin. A learned man. His closest Mason friend for many years. I believe that he was going to ask him to copy it. Yes, that's it." His face took on a puzzled expression. "But I had it committed to memory. Or at least I did at one time. Randall would regularly examine me on it. Knew each line, I used to know...each line."

"Did he tell you anything else?" Holmes asked.

The old man shook his head. "Only that he had to see Mr.Langhorn."

"Langhorn?"

"Yes," Thaddeus said, growing irritable. "Langhorn. The barrister."

"Whose barrister?"

"Randall's. He had to settle a debt. Over his gambling. Some very rough blokes were involved, you see." He seemed about to say more, and then his visage seemed to fade into uncertainty.

"Damn it all," the detective muttered.

"Holmes," I quickly interjected. "Sometimes a person with dementia can switch from the fog of intellectual deficit back to having a sharp, clear memory in a moment. Modern medicine can't explain it, but it is a fact."

"Yes, Watson," he said. "I'm aware of that."

Thaddeus was garrulous again, the words spilling out of him like water from a spout. "I told him to be careful. That man is in league with the Devil. I know that for sure, yes I do. The Devil, he is. He's with the Illuminati." The light in his eyes began to fade and his voice lowered to a gravely pitch. "Isn't that right, Samuel?"

Dr. Hester looked startled at being abruptly drawn into the conversation. He swallowed before speaking.

"Quite possibly, Pastor," he said, his voice laden with uncertainty. "Although it may be only a vicious rumor designed to smear the man's reputation."

"What?" Thaddeus said. "Poppycock. The Devil, I tell you. The Devil."

Dr. Hester glanced at me, raising his eyebrows to convey frustration.

"Yes, Thaddeus," he said. "The Devil himself."

"Indeed," Thaddeus continued, "Randall said that he owed Langhorn money from a case that Langhorn worked on a while ago for him. He said he was going to settle his debt."

"I've heard whispers of this Illuminati," Holmes said. "They fashion themselves to be a new world order. Supposedly involved secretly in politics and subterfuge at the highest levels. A power behind the throne, so to speak. If they really exist." Holmes lifted his index finger along his cheek bone and paused. "I wonder if the reason Tobias would have to visit such a man would be to trade him the information of the Secret Anthology in order to settle this debt?"

"Settle his debt," the old man said. "Yes, settle his debt. He was a gambler, you know."

The detective spun in his chair and clapped his hands together.

"So, Tobias gave the Secret Anthology to Polk to assist with a translation. Polk, who was also affiliated with the Templars, produced a copy of the pertinent pages and gave it to them, or possibly to Tobias, and now we have a barrister and possibly a third clandestine organization, the Illuminati, involved. And also remember that Tobias' last words were asking for Pastor Thaddeus to forgive him." He sprang to his feet. "Now we have the Masons in possession of the original Secret Anthology, the Templars in possession of a copy, and perhaps the Illuminati having a copy of Tobias' rendition of the contents. We have three murders and a treasure hunt, Watson."

Before Holmes could take a step, Thaddeus called out, "Be careful, good sir. The Secret Anthology will only bring death and destruction. The nail in the crown was responsible for killing the Lord Jesus. Don't let it do the same to you."

"Thank you for your concern, Pastor," Holmes said. "You have been quite helpful. We wish you good day, and shall leave you in peace."

Dr. Hester glanced at us both from his seat next to the door.

"I really must ask you not to return," he said. "I haven't seen him this agitated in quite some time."

"See here," I said. "I'll have you know that I'm a qualified physician, just as you are."

Dr. Hester's expression of anger hardened.

"The Pastor is my patient, sir," he said. "Not yours."

"I can assure you, Doctor, that we have no reason to return," Holmes interjected. "Now, come, Watson. We have a barrister to call upon to see where this Mr. Langhorn stands on the subject of crowns and nails."

CHAPTER 8

LLEWELLYN DAVIS LANGHORN, BARRISTER

Less than a half hour later the cab dropped us off before the law offices of Mr. Llewellyn Davis Langhorn on Rossmore Road. It was not all that far from Baker Street. Langhorn was rather well known in legal circles around London with many influential clients. His law offices were located on the second-floor of a rather quaint Georgian building. We made our way to the second-floor office of Langhorn and Cunningham, and Holmes gave his card to a middle aged, but smartly dressed, secretary who brought it into the inner office.

"Mr. Sherlock Holmes," came a hearty voice from within. "By all means, come in gentlemen."

We entered to find a large space occupied by a rather hefty man seated behind a desk, whom I could best describe as being dressed rather haphazardly. His right sleeve was slightly rolled up, his vest was unbuttoned at the top two button holes, and his tie dangled loosely in front of his many chins. And to top it off, his cheeks were flushed with a rosiness adding to a rather pink complexion. I suspected immediately that the man had a fondness for alcohol, and that, in turn had played havoc with his internal bodily functions. The medical man in me almost wanted to urge him to submit to a complete physical examination.

Standing next to him was a tall gentleman with an immaculate moustache, neatly clipped sideburns and a head of slicked back hair framing his sharp, angular face. I must say, they made quite the pair.

"Good afternoon," Holmes said, introducing himself. "As my card indicates, I am Sherlock Holmes, and this is my colleague, Dr. John H. Watson." He addressed the larger figure behind the desk. "And you are Mr. Langhorn, I presume."

"Yes, I am," came the reply. "This is my associate, Mr. Cunningham. What can I do for you, sirs?"

"Well, you could enlighten me about one of your clients," Holmes said.

"One of my clients?" The space between the large man's eyebrows formed twin creases and he cleared his throat. "And who might that be?"

"A Mr. Randall Tobias," Holmes said. "You see, I have some pressing legal business with him, and I was told that you represent him in all legal matters."

"You were told correctly, Mr. Holmes, is it?' He squinted down at the card. "That I do. Represent him, that is."

It was then that I noticed the half empty bottle of rye whiskey on the credenza behind him and the half full glass. There was only one glass, so it was obvious that only one of them was drinking and from the flush on the larger man's cheek, it was of little question who.

"In what matters do you represent him?" Holmes said. "I need to know if they conflict with my lawsuits against the man."

"I can't tell you that. It's a privileged client privilege," he slurred. "I can't say anything without Mr. Tobias's permission."

Holmes paused and stared directly into the other man's eyes.

"That might prove to be very difficult, Mr. Langhorn," Holmes said. "As your client is now dead."

He waited for the man's reaction.

I observed the expression of shock on Langhorn's face.

"Dead?" he said.

"Quite," Holmes said. "He was found murdered this very morning."

"Murdered? That can't be. Why I saw him just last Monday at about three in the afternoon." There was genuine shock in his voice as he dropped the business card on the desk. "Surely you jest."

"I assure you, I do not jest about such things. Now, I ask you again, in what matters do you represent him? Why was he here to see you?"

"Why he was just here to settle an old debt," Langhorn blubbered.

"Llewellyn," Cunningham said, "I think you've said enough."

As he moved over to place his hand on Langhorn's shoulder I caught sight of an intricate marble carving on the shelf behind him. It seemed to portray some sort of pyramid with some design encased inside of it in bas-relief.

"Mr. Langhorn," Holmes pressed. "What do you know of an Iron Crown?"

"Iron Crown," Langhorn muttered.

"Yes," Holmes said. "It's quite the antique, I'm told."

The other man's face reddened. "What about it?"

"You could tell me its whereabouts, for one thing," Holmes said. From the expression on the detective's face, I could tell that he was relishing his verbal sparring with this blustery barrister.

"Quite old." Langhorn blew out a derisive exhalation. "You blasphemer. What's this to you?" He shook his fist at the detective.

"Llewellyn!" Cunningham shouted. "That's enough."

He was now squeezing Langhorn's shoulder quite hard. "I'm going to insist that you both leave immediately or I will call the police."

"Ah, capital," Holmes said. "We happen to be working very closely with the police. I'm sure they'd be most eager to hear what you have to say."

Langhorn started to get up, but Cunningham shoved him back down.

"Mr. Holmes," he said. "We have nothing to say to them. Or you."

"Not even about the payment of an old debt?" Holmes raised an eyebrow in accompaniment to his smile as he stared down the other man.

No more words were spoken for several seconds until Holmes broke the silence.

"Very well, gentlemen," he said. "Thank you for your time. You've been most helpful," Holmes said and turned away. I quickly followed him out the door.

"That was rather exhilarating," said I, reaching the street. "It's too bad that they weren't more forthcoming."

Nevertheless," Holmes said. "The encounter was illuminating."

"It was?" I asked.

"Certainly," he said. "Did you happen to notice the marble carving on the shelf in back of Langhorn?"

"Of that pyramid with the design enclosed?" I answered. "One of the ugliest things I've ever seen."

"Hardly an innocent design, old boy," Holmes said. "It's the sign of the Illuminati."

"The Illuminati?"

He nodded. "The cryptic triangular design, enclosing the all-seeing eye, encased within the pyramid."

I was both astounded and embarrassed at having missed something of such significance. "That means what the pastor told us was correct."

"Yes, Watson. Another secret society enters the fray."

"Do you think they were the ones who murdered Tobias?"

The detective considered this for a long moment, and then shook his head. "Presumably not. Judging from Langhorn's reaction, it appeared that he didn't know that Tobias was dead; therefore it can be readily assumed that he had nothing to do with his murder. He is, however, definitely in the Illuminati, and he most assuredly knows about the Iron Crown. It's a fair assumption that he must have a copy of what Tobias related to him."

"As do we," I added.

"Quite," he said half in disgust. "At this rate, soon all of London will also have a copy."

"What do you plan to do next, Holmes?" I asked as I hailed a cab. The shadows were beginning to stretch out as the afternoon sun eased toward evening.

"I think we should go back to Baker Street and mull over the many avenues that this case has opened up to us. But first there is a stop I need to make."

"And where would that be?" I asked, as we climbed into the hansom.

"W. H. Dawe," he said.

The name had a ring of familiarity to me.

"The book seller?" I asked. Dawe's shop was on the corner next to 221B Baker Street. Holmes and I had been there many times.

"Yes," he said. "I need to pick up a few volumes of research on Masons, Templars and the Illuminati."

I chuckled. "Thinking of expanding your horizons and joining one of them?"

Holmes allowed himself a smile. "Let us just say that it will be my attempt to separate the facts from the fiction."

CHAPTER 9
ENTER THE THIEVES' GUILD

It was Thursday morning, a little after ten o'clock. I sat in my usual chair reading the *Daily Telegraph* police reports searching for anything of interest to pass on to Holmes. I found only the usual stories about muggings on the East End, several burglaries, two drunken brawls, two missing dogs, and the happy conclusion of one missing child case. Holmes, meanwhile, was hunched over at the table buried behind a pile of books with a copy of *M. Arthur Blackstone's Treatise on Surreptitious Societies and World Conspiracies* in his hands.

"Finding anything illuminating?" I asked, allowing the felicity to creep into my voice.

Holmes looked up and smiled. "This is fascinating, Watson. Did you know that the Illuminati are anti-clerical, anti-royal, and hold rational thought in the highest regard?"

I considered this and said, "Sounds a bit familiar at that."

Holmes laughed. "Yes, it does. Perhaps I've been a member of the Illuminati all along, and didn't know it."

"That is fascinating, Holmes. Now when we arrest the culprit for these three murders you can list the proper organization to which they belong on their police folder."

His head suddenly cocked to the side and he held up an index finger that curtailed further levity.

"Do you hear it?" he asked.

"Hear what?"

"Mrs. Hudson approaches."

And then the sound of her trudging up the seventeen steps became distinct to me.

"I'm afraid I've spent too much time on the battlefield to be that perceptive," I muttered.

"Time well spent," Holmes said, rising and placing the heavy book down on the table next to him. "For Queen and country, as well as all the wounded soldiers you helped in their moment of need."

My mind immediately flashed back to catching that Jezail bullet myself. It shattered the bone in my shoulder, nicked the subclavian artery, and ended up lodging in my leg. If it hadn't been for my faithful steward, Murray, I would have never made it back to the British lines.

The reverie was interrupted by the familiar knock upon our door.

"Yes, Mrs. Hudson." he said. "What is it?"

"There's an Inspector Gregson to see you, Mr. Holmes," she announced opening the door.

"Thank you, my dear," Holmes said, smiling. "If you would be so kind as to please show him in."

She vanished from the crevice and softly closed the door.

"Gregson," I said. "Now what in the Devil could bring him here?"

"Another murder, no doubt," Holmes said.

"How do you know that?"

"Elementary. Crime is a widening gyre, as Yeats put it. Once the dastardly deed has been consummated, it continues to spin, creating more havoc, more destruction until it is stopped." He paused and took in a deep breath before going to the mantel and retrieving his Persian slipper and cherry-wood pipe.

"It seems we've seen almost all of Scotland Yard so far this week," I said.

A few moments later, Inspector Gregson walked into our parlor. Tall, fair-haired with a chiseled chin, he openly acknowledged his admiration for Holmes' methods. He was fearless, never hesitating to charge in first, but could be callous at times. And occasionally he had a tendency to see things in shades of grey, not like the straight forward black and white absolutes of Lestrade's rigid perspective. Holmes often said of him that he was the smartest of the Scotland Yarders.

"Inspector Gregson, please do have a seat."

The inspector, who was a rather large-framed man, removed his hat and sat upon a nearby chair.

"Thank you," he said.

"Would you like a cup of tea?"

Gregson grunted an affirmation.

"Mrs. Hudson," Holmes shouted. "Would you be so kind as to prepare a cup of tea for the inspector?"

My ears pricked up at the sound of her footfalls on the steps. How the Devil Holmes had known she'd be listening on the other side of the door was beyond me. It set me wondering how many other times she'd been eavesdropping, but after all, it was her house.

Now," Holmes said. "What, may I ask, brings you to Baker Street on such a lovely morning?"

"A lovely morning for some, Mr. Holmes," Gregson said. "But not for others. It's official business, I'm afraid, and I'm in need of your opinion."

"Always happy to be of assistance," my friend said, as he crossed his legs and sat up in his chair. "Tell me all about it."

"There's been a murder at the Blue Ale Pub over on Terring Lane and Brinkstone Way. Happened about half past eleven last night."

Holmes smiled. "That can be a rather rough neighborhood, Inspector. If there is going to be a murder, I would expect it to be someplace like Terring Lane."

"Indeed," Gregson said. "That was my thought as well. At first it looked to be a simple tosser. They nicked the dead guy's wallet."

Holmes began packing his pipe with the tobacco from the slipper.

Gregson continued in his typical gruff voice. "A fancy barrister and his two mates were heading out of the local pub when they were jumped by a gang. There was a right fair donnybrook that went on for a minute or two. They gave as good as they got. But one of the barristers from the pub was stabbed with a knife and died quickly on the spot."

"This is all very interesting." Holmes struck a match and held it over the open portion of the pipe bowl. "And it concerns me how?"

"The victim was found with one of your cards in his possession. Llewellyn Langhorn."

If Holmes was surprised by this revelation, he didn't show it. He merely blew out a plume of pungent smoke and said, "How curious."

Gregson's features twitched with apparent confusion. That was apparently not the reaction he'd been hoping to get. "Well, you must admit, it's not often that the victim calls out for you from the dead. I came to question you about that."

Holmes seemed unfazed. "And I could tell you that there are many people in London who might be walking around with my card in their pocket at this very moment. But in this particular instance, I do know the man, having met him for the first time just yesterday. I was inquiring about a client of his. It concerned a case upon which I am currently working."

Gregson's brow furrowed. "Well, can you tell me what it is that you're working on?"

"Inspector, you know I cannot divulge the names of my clients. It wouldn't be ethical." He puffed some more on the pipe. "But perhaps I can enlighten you somewhat."

A hint of a smile graced Gregson's lips.

Holmes uncrossed his legs, sat erect with both feet on the floor, and steepled his hands in front of him, leaning in toward the inspector.

"Can you tell me a bit more about this altercation and murder?" Holmes asked.

"There wasn't much to be told by the scene," Gregson went on. "It was all scuff marks and dust from the battle. Witnesses said that the three thugs confronted the lawyers in question and began demanding some information. The scuffle broke out and got more intense. Two of the thugs drew knives and Mr. Langhorn was stabbed in the upper chest, near his heart, and died almost instantly. They nicked his wallet and then, after a tussle with the other two barristers, the three assailants fled. I interviewed everyone that I could."

"Did you obtain a good description of the assailants?" Holmes asked.

Gregson shrugged. "Not really so much. It was dark. Three toughs was all I got."

"And the other two barristers who were attacked?" Holmes said. "What were their names?"

"One was called Cording" Gregson said. "And the other was Cunningham."

"Yes, we met that Cunningham fellow yesterday," I said tilting my chair slightly to get out of the direct line of sunlight that was now pouring in through the window.

"Those two reluctantly corroborated the witnesses' description. But then they tried to deny that about Mr. Langhorn being very much in his cups and going on about some kind of silver crown," Gregson said. "But every witness I talked to confirmed it. He was bragging in the bar about some valuable magical crown, about a fortune in silver and jewels."

Holmes immediately dropped his hand to his chest and stared at the Inspector.

"Did you say a magic crown?" I asked.

"Yes," Gregson said. "As silly as that sounds. It makes no sense to me."

He paused and obviously stared at Holmes and myself as if trying to gauge our reactions to what he'd said. Despite Gregson's rather gruff appearance, the man was both cerebral and perceptive.

When neither Holmes nor I said anything more, he continued. "I was thinking that maybe somebody in the pub heard his ravings and went out and told the gang. Maybe they thought they had it with him. Or at least could lead them to where it was."

"Perhaps so," Holmes said.

"A silver crown," Gregson said with distain. "Priceless jewels. Sounds like something you'd read about in a fairy tale."

"A fairy tale indeed," Holmes said.

"That does sound a bit like the Mr. Langhorn we met," I interjected. "I could tell by the look of him that the man had a propensity for the overindulgence of alcohol."

Holmes appeared amused by my statement.

"Do enlighten us, old boy," he said.

"Well, it was his complexion, for one thing," I said. "His extreme corpulence for another. Why, if I were a betting man, I wouldn't have given him more than a few more years before he keeled over."

"That vicious gang didn't give him the chance, Doctor," Gregson said. "And despite the vagueness of the description, I have a pretty good idea of who they might be."

"Really?' Holmes asked settling back in his chair. "And who might that be?"

Gregson canted his head slightly and shot the detective a squint. "Ever hear of the Thieves' Guild?"

Holmes raised an eyebrow as he exhaled more smoke.

"Indeed," he said.

Before Gregson could continue I heard a tapping on the door.

Holmes turned to me.

"Watson, would you be so kind as to open the door for Mrs. Hudson?" he said. "I believe she's returned with the tea."

I rose and went to the door.

Sure enough, Mrs. Hudson stood there holding a tray with a teapot and three cups and saucers. A bowl of sugar sporting a dainty silver spoon and a smaller pot with cream in it sat off to the side.

I immediately took the tray from her and thanked her. I strode over to where Holmes and the inspector sat and placed the tray on the small table next to them. Then I picked up the pot and poured myself a cup, after placing it on a saucer. The scent of the fresh brew wafted delightfully upward and I found myself filled with relish.

"Every man for himself," I said, not wanting to play the part of a butler. As I resumed my seat I saw Gregson drop a spoonful of sugar and a copious amount of cream into his cup before filling it from the pot.

Holmes refrained from imbibing.

"You were about to inform us of your suspicions, Inspector," he said.

Gregson took a large gulp and grunted. "The Thieves' Guild. They're a crafty group of rogues who are very well organized. Run by a fellow who calls himself The Hawk. Nobody knows who this bloke is. They've been operating in the South End docks, and now in the West End recently." He drank some more tea and then frowned a bit, pausing in his recitation to add another spoonful of sugar before continuing. "They're a tight knit group of thieves who are quick thinking, cunning, and dangerous if they decide to be. They've been known to kill if they have to, just to make their score." Gregson drank from the cup again and this time smiled.

"Yes, Inspector," Holmes said. "I do believe I've read about them in the *Telegraph*. Some say they are a myth, do they not?"

Gregson snorted and slumped forward, causing some of his tea to slop over the side of his cup.

"No, sir, Mr. Holmes," he said. "You can take it to the bank that they aren't a myth. They're as real as the rain."

The detective smiled and nodded. "Others say they are the bane of Scotland Yard. I've never had the occasion to run into them in any of my cases." He removed the stem of the pipe from his mouth and allowed a thin stream of smoke to escape from his lips. "But perhaps the time has now come. We now have one criminal organization pitted against another secret organization. It seems to be a theme, eh, Watson?"

"What exactly do you mean by that, Holmes?" Gregson turned and eyed my companion sharply, seeking any new information about his case that he could glean.

Resting his forefinger on his chin, Holmes said, "I have it on good authority that your trio, Langhorn, Cording and Cunningham, were all members of a secret organization called the Illuminati."

Gregson's eyes narrowed. "The Illuminati?"

"Yes, this is information that would not be readily available to you. It appears that Langhorn's inability to control his drunken ramblings may have alerted those thieves to something more substantial than a mere wallet. I'm afraid that this spontaneous mugging may be connected to something much larger, and more sinister under the surface of things. The fact that he was murdered coming out of a pub speaking gibberish may be connected to the bigger picture. One that involves my inquiry."

"And what is that inquiry?" Gregson asked.

"Ah, Inspector, as I said, I can't divulge that privileged information. But if Scotland Yard has any information on the Illuminati I suggest that you include that in your investigation."

Holmes stood up and walked to the door and opened it. "This is the fourth death connected to this so-called magic crown. At least we know who the perpetrator of this one is."

"Holmes, four deaths ..." Gregson began. "You've got to tell me more."

"I'm afraid that I can't, Inspector," Holmes said. "At least not at this point. But I assure you that when I have anything more concrete I will be happy to share it with you. Suffice it to say that you know all of what I can tell you of my entire involvement with this Langhorn affair as pertains to his murder. As to the circumstances that are swirling around the edges of this, and my other case, you must allow me more time to compose my thoughts. Good day, Inspector."

Gregson knew that there was nothing more to say. He retrieved his hat, bid me good day, and left our room.

"Well, Watson, now we know that Langhorn's associates have a copy of the Secret Anthology thanks to the loose tongue of the late Mr. Langhorn. Randall Tobias did indeed give it to him to settle his debt."

"Do you think that they could make something out of the Anthology?"

"Most lawyers do have knowledge of Latin," said Holmes. "If they are clever enough they might be able to figure out that it is a coded map to a great relic. Anything is possible." Holmes stood there with his hand still on the door. "There is something that just occurred to me, however. I'll be back shortly."

He went down the stairs and outside. I moved to the bay window and pulled back the curtain and spied him standing on the stoop talking to a tall, slender lad in a tattered coat whose sleeves were too short for his long arms. Beside him were two other urchins, one in a newsboy cap and the other a curly-haired street urchin with a jacket one size too big for his tiny frame. Holmes gesticulated broadly. When he was finished, he withdrew several coins from his pocket and distributed them to the group. They nodded their appreciation and went flying off.

Within moments, he reentered our sitting room.

"Well, Holmes, what mission have you dispatched your street Arabs on now?"

"Street Arabs?" He chuckled. "I much prefer to call them the Baker Street Irregulars."

"Whatever," I said.

"The mission is a rather simple one, Watson. They are to spread the word that I wish all of them to keep an ear out for any news on the street concerning the Masons or the Templars. It took a little longer to explain to them who Masons and Templars are, but I am sure that they have a grasp

I spied him standing on the stoop talking to a tall, slender lad in a tattered coat .

of the concept now."

Holmes walked over to the fireplace and picked up his long-stemmed black clay pipe from the mantle and grabbed another pinch of tobacco from his Persian slipper.

"I also told them to find out what they could about this fellow who calls himself The Hawk," Holmes said.

I glanced at the table and saw that his cherry wood pipe still lay there, but its embers were now extinguished. My friend was intent on his mental calculations

Holmes carefully stuffed the bowl and took a match from the box on his desk. He puffed smoothly to catch the small flame, shook out the match and tossed it into the cold firebox.

"I believe that I shall spend the rest of the day engaged with the books I purchased last night to absorb the secrets of the past that have carried our players into the present."

"Sounds like a worthy ambition for the day," I said. "And I do have some patients to look in on."

"Did you know, Watson, that the Illuminati are originally a Bavarian organization formed to promote enlightened ideas among the elite? They sprung out of Free Mason lodges. Somehow they evolved into a group that plants agents in all levels of government to secretly guide them into acting in the manner that they desire." He shot me a quick wink and a grin. "Allegedly, of course."

"Of course," I said, as I lit my thin cigar. "Fascinating, Holmes. And that includes 10 Downing Street?"

"Undoubtedly." His grin widened. "But I shall be principally concentrating on whether the Iron Crown was donated by the Pope in 628 to Monza outside of Milan or whether it stayed in Constantinople and was lost when the city was looted in 1204. I must then trace the clues written down in Latin in the Secret Anthology. That should occupy my time, wouldn't you say?"

"Yes. And as I said, I think I'll drop in on a few patients who I haven't seen in a while and check up on them."

"Until later then," he said. "Godspeed."

Chapter 10
The Guild Strikes

It was a quarter past five when I returned to Baker Street and ascended the stairs. As I entered our sitting room, I was surprised to find Inspector Gregson seated on our sofa, his legs crossed, engaged in a conversation with Holmes.

"And that's—"

Gregson stopped in mid-sentence and glanced at me.

"Do come in, Watson," Holmes said. "You're just in time. The inspector's just arrived and was beginning to tell me of the latest development in the Langhorn case. Do start over, Inspector."

Gregson cleared his throat. "Well, as I was telling Mr. Holmes here, about two hours ago there was a brazen break-in on Rossmore Road to the offices of the late Mr. Langhorn. It could only have been the Thieves' Guild. Four of them came bursting in on Cunningham, Cording and another fellow named Hoople. According to Mr. Cunningham, they were wearing burlap sacks over their heads, with eye holes cut out, to hide their faces. First they slashed the arm of the poor secretary in the outer office and shoved her into the corner. Then they surrounded the three barristers in the main office. The nearest I can figure is that they had one of their confederates follow Cunningham back home last night after the bar fight and then tailed him to his office this morning after they rounded up their gang."

"This group of ruffians is sounding more dangerous with each passing moment," I said.

Gregson nodded and continued. "Just like in the brawl last night, Cunningham and Cording put up a pretty good fight, but they were no match for knives and cudgels. They carved up Hoople real bad, and beat Cording. But during the fight, Cording managed to yank the hood off of one of their faces and saw the assailant had a handlebar moustache and a nasty scar above his left eye high up above his eyebrow. Then they put Cunningham in his chair and he said they tortured him for information on some trial that was coming up."

The Inspector reached into his jacket pocket and drew out a packet of cigarettes. He pulled one out.

"At least that was the story they gave to the first Bobbies on the scene." He stuck a cigarette between his lips, flicked a match, lighted it, and then sat back with the knowing smirk of a Cheshire cat.

"But I got the real story out of the secretary," he said. "Before they took her to the hospital she told me she heard the assailants yelling at Cunningham about some silver crown and some jewels. I'm beginning to think this magic silver crown is real."

"Oh, I can assure you, Inspector," Holmes said, "there are people who believe it is. Please continue."

"Cunningham said that he didn't tell them anything about this supposed trial, and when I confronted him about what his secretary had told me, the bugger denied that they ever asked about any such magic crown. He said they finally just broke his arm, grabbed as much stuff from the office that seemed valuable, and left."

"Why would Cunningham lie to you about what had occurred?" I asked.

Gregson shrugged. "Lying to the police is a way of life for those barristers. So, Mr. Holmes, is there something to this crown business?"

"It would seem so, Inspector."

Gregson considered this, blew out some smoke, and asked, "Do I have to start investigating the Illuminati? It's harder to find out anything about them than it is to find out information about the blasted Thieves' Guild."

"I would put Scotland Yard on notice if I were you," Holmes said. "I think you are going to be hearing a lot more from the Thieves' Guild. As for the actual existence of this crown, that is still in question. But as for this Cunningham not knowing anything about the supposed crown, I know for a fact that he is lying. If Langhorn knew about its rumored existence, then Cunningham did too. He surely wants to protect the knowledge of its supposed existence. For him and his compatriots to endure a beating, much less go to the great length of sustaining a broken arm, to maintain his secrecy, says a lot about the lengths they will go to protect the secret."

Gregson sat there, his cigarette smoldering in hand, most probably trying to figure out if the crown was real or not.

"Holmes, it's not good for my case or for Scotland Yard to have brutal attacks and robberies like this in broad daylight," he said. "And on prominent barristers to boot. All for some crown that may or may not exist?"

"If I may I rely on your discretion, Inspector," Holmes said. "I would ask that you try to downplay any mention of the crown's part in this affair as much as possible. Tell the newspapers that it was precious jewelry that they were after, or some such."

"I got it," Gregson said. "Not releasing everything to the press so we can separate the grain from the chaff." He drew upon his cigarette and let the smoke seep out with his next words. "I'll keep the crown out of it. For now."

As if on cue, from outside our window, we could hear on the street below the voice of the newspaper vendor cry out, "Lawyers office robbed. Lawyer attacked. Drawing of attacker here."

"Well, at least I didn't hear anything about a crown," I said. "Or the Illuminati."

Gregson nodded appreciatively as he puffed on his cigarette.

"So what should my next move be, Holmes?" the inspector asked.

"Rest assured you will have the barristers using their contacts from the underworld of scoundrels and toughs whom they have defended in the past as their retaliatory agents. Once that occurs, you will no doubt have an underworld war of attrition on your hands."

Gregson's expression hardened. "I don't like the sound of that one bit."

"That has to nipped in the bud," I exclaimed. "There's no telling how much carnage that could cause. And it would be bound to escalate."

"Your next move, Inspector," said Holmes, "should be to continue to delve into the identity of this Thieves' Guild and its leader, and remove them from the equation as soon as possible. Up until now, Scotland Yard has not been able to do much of that. I suggest that you also have your men keep an eye on the remaining barristers in the Langhorn group of Illuminati and their associates. If you can cut off any action on their part that would surely help allay the situation."

Gregson took one final inhalation on his cigarette and then looked around for a place to stub it out.

"I'll take that," I said, rising and holding out my hand.

He placed the smoldering butt between my fingers and I tossed it into the fireplace. Once more in momentary contemplation, I considered giving up the use of tobacco completely, so vile was the odor of Gregson's foul-smelling cigarette.

Perhaps another time, I told myself and turned back to him and Holmes.

"Thank you, Mr. Holmes," Gregson said. "Rest assured I shall continue to keep you apprised of any further developments."

Holmes smiled and gave him a playful clap on the shoulder.

The inspector grinned. "And I thought I had a simple mugging with your business card attached."

"Will wonders never cease?" Holmes said, escorting him to the door. "Good evening, Inspector."

As we heard Gregson descending the stairs, Holmes exclaimed, "I say, that newspaper boy just gave me a wonderful idea."

He sprinted down the stairs and out onto the stoop. I went to the window and watched as below he glanced around and finally waved down four of his Baker Street Irregulars. He squatted down and gave them a long set of instructions. Then he gave them what appeared to be several pound notes apiece and pointed to the corner. I saw them scamper to the news vendor and begin to buy up every copy of the evening *Globe* that they could carry.

Holmes entered our parlor with a look of extreme satisfaction on his face.

"What better way to send the boys out to reconnoiter than to give them a picture of their target." He held up the folded newspaper so that I could see the artistic rendition of the tough looking visage, replete with a scar above his left eye. "I've just sent them on a mission to ferret out our Thieves' Guild attacker whose picture is being circulated in the paper."

"Brilliant, Holmes," I said. "Almost as good as circulating a photograph."

Immediately behind him, Mrs. Hudson poked her head in and said, "If it's all right with you, gentlemen, I'll bring your supper up now."

"Oh, Mrs. Hudson," my friend growled, "I've no time for a trifle like supper. I've got to get back to my studies. How can I get anything done with these constant interruptions?"

"I'll be happy to enjoy your wonderful meal," I said politely.

"Thank you, Doctor," she smiled at me and then gave a stern look to Holmes before starting down the stairs.

"You really should make an effort to be more polite," I said.

"What?" Holmes said, already sorting through his stack of books. "Oh, do tell her to leave my food on the tray and I'll get to it later."

"Righto, old chap," I said.

I looked forward to her dinner. My companion was already seated in his chair, the same heavy volume on the Crusades now propped up in his lap, head down, and completely absorbed in the 13th century.

I couldn't help but smile at his single-mindedness and the sight made me glad that he had become so immersed in this current conundrum as to occupy his brilliant mind.

As I shuffled toward the table I told myself, better him than I.

Chapter 11
Death at the Stable

It was barely half past seven on an overcast Friday morning when I heard Mrs. Hudson knocking forcefully on our sitting room door across the hall from my bedroom. I had just finished shaving and was about to put on my jacket. I paused to wonder why she was bringing our breakfast up so early. I cracked open my door to hear her say in an agitated voice, "Dr. Watson, please inform Mr. Holmes that one of his vagrant children is at the door insisting to see him. He says it's a matter most urgent."

"Show him in, Mrs. Hudson," I heard Holmes call out.

She frowned. "Very well. I shall. But keep your eye on the little bugger, Doctor. Heaven knows what his unsavory little hands might latch onto."

I assured her that I would.

"I don't know what could be so urgent at this hour," she muttered as she turned to go back down the stairs.

"The urgency of my cases is none of your concern," Holmes shouted out.

I quickly closed the door, hoping it would obfuscate his discourteous retort.

"Holmes," I said. "As I told you yesterday, you really should endeavor to show our land lady a bit more courtesy."

"My dear Watson," he replied, still out of view in the other room. "I have no time or inclination to be concerned about social amenities when there are lives at stake. Please bring the boy in here."

"We'll be lucky if she doesn't raise the rent," I muttered and peered out through the sliver of opening between the door and the jamb. I saw her walking behind a bedraggled youth clad in a filthy, over-sized coat with frayed cuffs. The boy's shoes looked so worn that I could see the folds of newspaper sticking out between the separated juncture of sole and shoe. Opening the door to admit him, I caught the unpleasant scent of the unwashed. From the unmistakably petulant expression on her face, I instantly knew that Mrs. Hudson had no doubt caught the same pungent, odiferous waft of the boy's body odor that I had.

I thanked her and reluctantly placed a hand on the youth's shoulder in a gesture designed to connote my diligent regard to her request for assiduous vigilance. Beneath the garment I could feel his bony frame and little else.

I waited until Mrs. Hudson had started back down the stairs to usher the lad in to sneak across the landing and enter our rooms. I found Holmes draped across the very same chair where I had left him the previous evening. He looked disheveled, obviously having gotten no sleep. The tray of food brought by Mrs. Hudson the evening before looked untouched.

"Good morning, Holmes," said I. "Did you sleep well?"

"Humor eludes you, Watson." His face looked drawn and tight and the whites of both of his eyes were strewn with threads of redness.

"You know," he said, "I was originally reading this extremely interesting book on the Crusades. Unfortunately, I followed it up with *The Unknowable Sands of Time: The Secrets Beneath the Reasons of Symbols and Societies Unknown*. By God, man, the author should be buried beneath those sands of time. Such awful prose and misguided logic should never have seen the light of day."

He threw the book down on the floor.

The slender boy jumped back with a start.

His obvious trepidation seemed to shake Holmes out of his rant. His face softened into a smile and he said, "Ah, Wiggins, come in, lad. What do you have for me?"

The boy swallowed as he stepped forward.

"Well, Mr. Holmes, we been out on the looksies for that bloke you showed in the newspapers yesterday. The one with the scar about his eye, that is."

Holmes leaned forward with an eagerness. "And you found him?"

"Not exactly," Wiggins said. "But Bertie Budd thought you might want to know that there was a big fight early this morning down at the stables on Clarke Street."

Holmes' brow furrowed. "A fight?"

"Yes, sir. A big one. Bertie saw it all. Two gents got killed. Both by knives. Two more got injured. What Bertie heard when they was fighting is that they called each other a Mason and a Temple man."

Holmes raised an eyebrow as he reached inside his pants pocket. "Excellent work, my boy. On Clarke Street, you say? Here, Wiggins, an extra sovereign for you and one for Bertie. Keep up the good work. Keep your ears to the streets for more."

I escorted the boy to the door and was about to call out to Mrs. Hudson when I saw her standing mid-way on the seventeen steps of the stairway.

I flashed as beatific a smile as I could and told her the young man would be leaving.

Her lower lip was jutting out in disapproval as she gesticulated for young Wiggins to descend. I closed the door quietly.

"Watson, we must be off at once," Holmes said. With that, he bolted up and grabbed his top hat and headed for the door. "This should prove to be a most interesting development."

We arrived at the stables on Clarke Street in less than fifteen minutes just beating the steady rise of the morning's customary heavy traffic of buggies and carriages. There was a crowd gathered around the outer pens all craning their necks for a look at what the constables were doing inside the stables. We wound our way through the throng and, arrived at the front of the assembly. The first thing we saw were several Bobbies standing guard over two lifeless bodies covered by small canvas tarps. Other Yarders had corralled several men in tousled and torn state of dress, ripped bloody shirts and cut arms and faces. But to our surprise, we found both Inspector Lestrade and Inspector Hopkins standing there arguing with each other.

Both Holmes and I walked over to them carefully avoiding the dead bodies. "Good morning, Inspectors," my friend said. "It seems there was a dance scheduled for this early morning. I do hope I'm not too late for it."

"Holmes," Lestrade exclaimed. "What the Devil are you doing here?"

"Mr. Holmes, I was just thinking about contacting you," Hopkins said. "I wonder if this is somehow connected with the case that we are working on together."

This admission seemed to raise Lestrade's ire.

"What case are you working on with Holmes?" demanded Lestrade. "He's working on a sensitive case with me."

"He and I happen to be working on my case with the Masons," Hopkins said in refute. "And this brawl involves the Masons."

Lestrade puffed up his chest and stuck it out at the taller Hopkins. "Now see here. This is an incident involving the Templars. And Mr. Sherlock Holmes is assisting *me* with a Duke and the Templars."

"Gentlemen," my companion said as he stepped forward." I believe there is enough of me, so to speak, to go around. I am quite able to assist both of you."

This seemed, for the moment, to quiet the dispute between the two inspectors.

Holmes glanced at each of them in turn, and then smiled disarmingly.

"Let's see what we have here," he said. "It appears that both of your cases have coalesced into this volatile and ongoing conflict between the Masons and Templars. Now, if one of you would be so kind as to fill me in on exactly what transpired here, we can begin to sort out the particulars of this troublesome affair."

They both began at once.

"Well, Mr. Holmes—"

"But, Holmes, the case—"

Holmes held up his arms.

"Gentlemen, one at a time please. Inspector Lestrade, you may go first."

"Thank you." He shot a look of stern reproach toward Hopkins, which was subsequently replaced with an expression of satisfaction that crossed his narrow, pointed face. "About half past six this morning these Masons here supposedly came to the Templars' stables looking to talk about horses. The Templars were apparently minding their own business when this all started. It seems some harsh words were exchanged. One thing led to another and before long the fists started flying. And then, the knives came out. The first one to get it was that Mason over there." He pointed to one of the bodies under the tarp. "A Mr. Pounder."

I glanced down at the tarp, cognizant that I knew the fellow underneath it.

"The next one to get it," Lestrade continued, "was this Templar fellow, Hager. He took a knife to the throat. Real messy."

Lying to my left was a soul who had been most helpful to us when we first met. I have no doubt that he was only doing his duty at the stable when the violence occurred.

What a waste, I thought.

"I've got more information than that," Hopkins said. "And the motive, too."

"I'm not done talking yet," Lestrade snapped.

"You've talked enough already," Hopkins barked back impatiently.

"Please," my friend said. "Let Lestrade finish with his account."

"Thank you." Lestrade glared at his fellow inspector, and then cleared his throat. "The rest of the Masons are sitting over there. A pretty tight lipped group, they are, but I got out of them that they came down here to discuss business with the Templars about horses. As I said, but the Templars didn't like the deal that they were offering and insulted them."

"That's a load of horse shite," Hopkins snarled. "I've got the true reasons that this donnybrook transpired, Mr. Holmes."

I was shocked at Hopkins's vulgarity.

Apparently he was as well, for his cheek showed a sudden subsequent flush of crimson.

He drew himself straight in an obvious effort to try to show up Lestrade.

"And it's the truth of the matter," he said. "Since I've dealt with these Masons before, I have a better sense on how to get information out of them. Apparently, this gang of Masons was led by this Pounder fellow, and was sent down here to exact revenge on the Templars for the murder of one, Mr. Randall Tobias, who was one of their own. It was one gang against the other with a motive as old as the Bible itself. An eye for an eye."

"The killing of Tobias is *my* case," Lestrade yelled. "What are you doing poaching my case? You keep out of my investigation, Hopkins."

"Balderdash, Lestrade," Hopkins retorted. "It just so happens that Tobias was the prime suspect in the fire and theft of some valuable papers from the Masonic Temple. So I'll thank you not to interfere with *my* investigation."

"*Your* investigation." Lestrade's glare looked ferocious. "Now see here—"

Hopkins hardly seemed intimidated, however. He burst in again. "No, *you* see here. Why didn't you inform me about the death of this Tobias fellow? It was common knowledge around the Yard that I was seeking him out."

"Why …" Lestrade sputtered. "It was in some of the newspapers."

"Well, I don't get requested information regarding an ongoing police investigations by reading the newspapers, Lestrade," Hopkins shot back. "It seems you were violating proper Scotland Yard protocol."

Lestrade's mouth gaped slightly. "Horse feathers. I was doing nothing of the kind."

"Inspectors, please," Holmes said, trying to calm the situation. "You both have an interest in Mr. Tobias and both of these organizations. Let's leave it at that for the moment, shall we?"

"What do you mean, Mr. Holmes?" Hopkins asked.

"I mean that I shall explain it all shortly if given a chance. I have some new information concerning Tobias and the Secret Anthology that will help clear up a few items in your case, Hopkins. I'll tell you about them later this morning."

"Wait just one minute," said Lestrade. "Just what brought you down here so early, Holmes? This matter isn't even in any newspapers yet. The news reporters ain't even been here."

Holmes let a crafty smile twitch the corners of his lips.

"Quite true, Lestrade," he said. "But I have many eyes and ears on the streets of London and beyond that keep me informed as to the goings on of certain matters."

"And you can take that to the bank," I added for emphasis.

Lestrade's lower lips encroached upon his bushy mustache. "Be that as it may, you being here strikes me as a bit peculiar."

"If not prescient," Hopkins added.

That the two adversarial inspectors now seemed united in their suspicion of him seemed to give Holmes a bit of amusement. He laughed aloud.

"Gentlemen, please. As I told you, I am working on cases that the both of you are involved in concerning the Masons and the Templars," said Holmes. "And I have my ways of knowing what goes on in London that is beyond the scope of police intelligencia. Now, it seems as if the two of you would be able to finish up here nicely, if you stop tripping over each other's shoes. After that, I would like to see you both at Baker Street at about ten this morning. I assure you, it will be worth your while."

"Then you'll be helping me sort this out," Lestrade said eagerly.

"But, Mr. Holmes." Hopkins forcefully raised his carriage up to his full height so that he could look down on Lestrade. "You said you would be helping me with my investigation. I'm working under strict supervision of the Chief Constable, himself."

Lestrade snorted. "Go back and tell the Chief Constable what you got, which is nothing."

Hopkins flushed. "You're the one who's got less than nothing. Why, I was working this one first—"

"Please," Holmes interjected. "Let us all seek some common ground here." He paused and waited while both men glared at each other in silence. "Now, as I suggested, finish up here, and be at Baker Street at ten o'clock." The detective shook his head and turned away to make his way back through the crowd that had gotten larger.

I hustled to catch up to him. "I say, Holmes, this is murder number five and six connected with the Masons and the Templars. The bodies are piling up, aren't they?"

Holmes heaved a heavy sigh. "It is indeed a tangled web we weave, Watson. Beginning with a Secret Anthology."

"I'd almost forgotten about that," I said. "A tangled web … that's from Shakespeare, isn't it?"

He nodded and then said, "And it's also one that we had better start to unweave, lest more bodies begin to fall."

Chapter 12
Meeting of the Minds

On the way back Holmes stopped at a local post and sent a message to Inspector Gregson inviting him to the same meeting at ten o'clock that morning at our quarters. A cool morning breeze greeted us as the sun began to burn away the morning clouds as we reached our Baker Street lodgings. I had been mulling over his instructions the entire way and couldn't, for the life of me, figure out what he could possibly have in mind by summoning all three of the inspectors to the same meeting.

"So tell me, Holmes," I finally said. "Exactly what is this meeting going to be about?"

He opened the door and held it for me to enter first. "I think it's high time that we brought all three inspectors into our confidences on the particulars of the case so that we are all working on the same page."

"The case," I said. "You used the singular. Is it your conjecture that all of these instances are in fact related then?"

He cast me a rather reproachful glance as we began to ascend the stairs.

"May I remind you, Watson, that I never merely conjecture. I access all the known facts, assemble them in the most likely scenario, and eliminate the impossible. Whatever remains, no matter how improbable, is the answer."

"Quite," I said. "I shall have to remember that for my recounting of this case."

"We shall discuss that later as well, old boy. Now, in the meantime, we must tread very carefully with our three guests. Any one of them may stumble over something useful to us, quite by accident most probably, but none the less, we have Withermew's and Polk's and now Tobias's murder to solve. All of these others factors are as incidental to our case as supernumeraries in a theater production."

We entered our rooms and took our familiar seats at the table. Just as I'd picked up the morning paper, Holmes sprang to the door even before there came a knocking. He opened it and Mrs. Hudson brought in our delayed breakfast. The eggs were slightly cold but the several biscuits and jam were wonderful and the tea was hot. I picked up the morning *Times*. Holmes took a few bites out of his biscuit and immediately pounced into his chair and opened another of his recently purchased books. This one was a dust-covered, red leather volume about translating Latin into English.

"Makes one wish he'd paid more attention in school," I joked. "Doesn't it?"

"Indubitably," he said. "It's an ancient language with which I am more than slightly familiar, but obviously I am in the need of sharpening my skills due to the lack of practice in the intervening years since my childhood studies."

He slathered a bit more butter on the remainder of his morsel and I knew right then that I would have an extra biscuit for myself.

Before I realized it, the clock was striking ten—the assigned time for our meeting with the three inspectors.

Inspector Hopkins arrived first and I had settled in with our guest when I heard two carriages pull up in front of our flat followed by a pounding on the front door. Mrs. Hudson's voice was prominent in the subsequent fray, insisting that she announce the presence of any guests.

"Stand aside, madam," I heard Gregson's bass voice trumpet. "I'm here to see Mr. Sherlock Holmes and this is official Scotland Yard business."

Our landlady's near shriek was followed by the sound of two sets of footsteps racing up the steps. There was a quick knock on the door.

"Come in, gentlemen," said Holmes, who then looked at me. "Watson, be a good old fellow and go down to smooth the no doubt ruffled feathers of our landlady."

"No doubt," I said.

"And also do ask her if she'd be good enough to prepare a pot of tea for our guests."

"You don't expect much," I said allowing the trace of sarcasm to invade my tone. "Do you?"

"We must remember to take measures to treat her with more deference, old boy," Holmes answered, flashing a wicked grin. "Now do open the door, please."

Before I could make my way over there, the door flew open and Inspector Gregson, being the larger and more fit between himself and Inspector Lestrade, elbowed his way into our lodgings. Behind him Lestrade, who was of smaller frame, struggled mightily to squeeze past him. There was a look of embarrassment on Gregson's face when he saw that Inspector Hopkins was already seated on the sofa.

"Do come in, gentlemen, "Holmes said. "Please find a chair." He pointed around the room with the stem of his cherry wood pipe.

"What is the meaning of this, Holmes?" Gregson blurted out. "Why would you call all of us here? Especially these two."

"I wasn't aware that *you* were invited," Hopkins said.

"I'm too busy to sit around here with the likes of these—" Lestrade began to protest.

Holmes raised his hands and smote them together in a resounding clap. It had the intended effect to silence the entire room.

"Calm down, gentlemen," Holmes said in a commanding tone. "All will be explained. But first, please allow Dr. Watson to use his charm with the fairer sex to soothe the no doubt roused umbrage of our precious landlady, to whom you were most rude and presumptuous."

The two police inspectors mumbled to themselves, but each took a seat.

"Ah," Holmes said. "That's so much better. Now perhaps a bit of tobacco will ease the tension a bit further. Watson, do see about that tea."

I went down the stairs and found Mrs. Hudson in a tizzy. She dabbed at her cheeks with a handkerchief.

"There, there, Mrs. Hudson," I said. "I come to convey the deepest apologies for the abrupt conduct of our guests."

She pursed her lips and shook her head.

"Oh, Dr. Watson, you are a true gentleman, coming to check on me this way."

After a few more choice words I conveyed our request for tea and she seemed more than happy to comply.

"Do you wish me to wait here so that I can take it up myself?" I asked, hoping that she would decline my offer so that I could get back up to the meeting.

"No, doctor, I'll bring it up myself in a bit."

With that, I turned and rushed up the stairs as judiciously as I could, not wanting to revisit the clamorous assent to which she had just witnessed. Inside I found Holmes and the three guests in the sitting room enveloped in a haze of tobacco smoke. The smell was such that I removed my own pipe and began packing the bowl.

"Now that Dr. Watson has returned," Holmes said, pointing the stem of the long pipe in my direction, "would each of you be good enough to tell me where you are currently in your investigations?"

The three of them stared warily at each other, showing that the reticence was unanimous.

"Come, come," Holmes said. "We do need to move forward. Lives are at stake."

Gregson cleared his throat and began. "I have the Yarders scouring the streets for any signs of the Thieves' Guild. We've gone through our police files again looking at recent burglaries to see if any of those apprehended can be traced back to them."

"The Thieves' Guild," Lestrade muttered. "No one told me that they were involved."

Gregson started to reply, but Holmes made a tsking sound and shook his head.

The headmaster in charge of his recalcitrant students, I thought with a bit of glee.

"We've also increased patrols in the West End neighborhood districts," Gregson continued. "That's where the more affluent homes are. We want to see if we can catch any of these buggers in the act. I also have all my network of Bobbies in the area listening for any rumors on any illicit activity."

He finished his pronouncements and crossed his arms over his chest, his expression triumphant.

"An excellent idea," Holmes said. "Not quite as efficient as my own network, but an admirable effort none the less."

"They're sure to strike again soon," Gregson continued ignoring Holmes' comment. "And when they do, we'll be ready to snatch them up. If there's a prize like this silver crown dangling out there in front of them, they'll be tempted for sure."

"Silver crown?" Hopkins said, his face showing incredulity.

Holmes waggled his index finger dismissively.

"Thank you, Inspector Gregson," he said. "Now, Inspector Lestrade, if you please."

"Well, I've been doing some real detective work," Lestrade crowed, eager to get into the conversation, "Keeping my eye on those Templar fellows. I got my boys tailing the higher up muckers, recording their comings and goings. They won't be so high and mighty once I catch them red-handed killing another Mason. Dumping a body in the alley and calling it diplomatic immunity," he huffed. He ran his thumb up and down the braces on his trousers to emphasize his accomplishment. "And that quarrel at the stables, that was probably connected to a bit of retaliation involving my case with that Tobias fellow."

"Oh?" Hopkins said sarcastically. "Now you think it's about revenge, and not horse trading, do you?"

"And diplomatic immunity?" Gregson chortled. "What in God's name are you babbling on about now, Lestrade?"

Lestrade straightened up in his seat. "It's something they claimed at the onset," he stated quite emphatically. "Right out of the gate."

"The only thing out of the gate is you, Lestrade," Gregson said. "How can you let anyone pull something like that one over on you?"

"I didn't say that they pulled anything over on me," Lestrade shot back. "I said they tried to. But I was too smart to fall for that load of manure. Me and Mr. Holmes, here."

"Well, you certainly were shoveling a lot of manure this morning," Hopkins said brushing his moustache.

"At least I don't have the Chief Constable constantly looking over my shoulder on my case, Hopkins," Lestrade retorted.

Holmes clapped his hands together once more and a short silence fell over the room.

"Gentlemen, we're wasting time with this bickering," Holmes said in a stern voice. "May I suggest we continue? Hopkins, what have you been doing?"

Before the final inspector of the trio could reply, I heard Mrs. Hudson's familiar knocking on the door.

"There's the tea, no doubt," I said.

"Capital," Holmes said. "Perhaps each of you should consider an extra teaspoon of sugar to temper your obstreperousness."

He eyed each of them in turn, and the three sets of eyes immediately focused on the floor.

I rose and met Mrs. Hudson at the door. She insisted on bringing the tray with the teapot, cups, and saucers into the room. Her reproachful gaze centered on both Gregson and Lestrade, who had both pushed past her.

"Mrs. Hudson," Holmes said. "These two gentlemen both wish to apologize to you for their rudeness a little while ago." He raised both eyebrows as he stared from Gregson to Lestrade. "Isn't that correct?"

Both of them muttered some virtually unintelligible sentences of remorse. To Mrs. Hudson's ears, however, the apologies seemed satisfactory. She smiled and nodded an acknowledgement to Holmes and then left the room. All three of the inspectors busied themselves with fixing themselves cups of tea.

Holmes waited until they'd all administered their milk and sugar, and then pointed at Hopkins.

"Proceed with your account," he said.

"Mr. Holmes," Hopkins started, "I'm still investigating any enemies

"Gentlemen, we're wasting time with this bickering."

whom the Masons might have, who would want to do harm to Dr. Withermew and steal the Anthology." He paused to take a copious bit of the liquid. "But may I ask, whom do you think was the second hooded figure who in probably started the fire in the library?"

"At this point," Holmes said, "we have no solid evidence on that. What else have you got?"

"Well, I'm still trying to figure out how this all ties in with the death of Battalion Chief Polk. How did he get the original copy of the Secret Anthology? Now I have the murder of Randall Tobias. Every day, it seems, I'm saddled with more questions than answers."

"Well, Hopkins," Holmes said. "I can give you some answers to your questions."

Hopkins set his cup and saucer down on the small table and leaned forward.

"As supplied by Pastor Thaddeus," Holmes said. "To whom Tobias was in the practice of confessing. Tobias urged Withermew to allow him to hide the Secret Anthology in a more secure location. Thus, it had to be the second hooded man who killed Dr. Withermew. Tobias took the Secret Anthology to Polk's, allegedly in an attempt to decipher its meaning, which Tobias was attempting to do with the help of his mentor, Thaddeus. Polk hid the Anthology in one of his fireman's boots. One can only speculate that the second hooded fellow from the fire was the one who somehow discovered this and killed Polk in the process of looking for the Secret Anthology.

"For some reason," Holmes continued, "Polk made a copy of one page in particular of the Anthology, and sent it off to the Templars. And that is where Randall Tobias' body was found."

"Which is my case," Lestrade said.

Holmes, whom I knew detested being interrupted, clipped any further retort by virtue of a piercing stare. After a moment, he continued.

"But on Monday last, Tobias went to see his barrister, Mr. Langhorn, a member of another secret organization known as the Illuminati. This is for your benefit Inspector Gregson," Holmes turned to address him directly. "And at this time Tobias told Langhorn about the existence of this Secret Anthology, which, indeed, does hold the possible clues to a treasure of a royal silver crown."

"And why did he do that?" Gregson asked.

"The initial explanation," Holmes said, "was that he was doing it in consideration of the payment of an outstanding debt. I have no evidence to dispute the veracity of this theory, although I suspect that Tobias, who had a well known propensity for gambling, may have had a financial incentive, one that was supplied by Langhorn, to divulge this information."

"But if the Anthology was still in Polk's possession," Gregson said. "What good would just telling him about it be?"

"Pastor Thaddeus related that he had committed certain portions of the Anthology to memory," Holmes said. "As his memory began to fail, the old man induced his protégé, Tobias, to do the same. Thus, Tobias was possibly able to recreate the pertinent pages that were being sought by the Illuminati."

"So they all know where this crown is at?" Lestrade asked.

Holmes shook his head. "The location has not remained a secret for centuries by serendipity. No, the location is no doubt shrouded within some sort of complex riddle that has yet to be deciphered."

"Which no one has been able to do for quite some time," I added. "If at all."

"So this fellow Langhorn was killed because he knew the location?" Gregson asked.

"Hardly," Holmes said. "He was a boastful braggart and it was his drunken ramblings at the pub that got him killed by the Thieves' Guild, who are also after the crown. That is how your case is tangentially connected."

"So there is a silver crown connected with all of this," Gregson said excitedly like a boy just opening his Christmas gift. "But no one knows where it's at?"

"Precisely. The Secret Anthology holds the clues to its location. It's a treasure map of sorts." Holmes rose from his chair and tapped the extinguished embers from his pipe into the fireplace. He then repacked the bowl with more tobacco and retrieved a box of matches from the drawer of his desk. Grabbing a match, he struck and lit it. "Lestrade, I don't have enough information at this time to tell you how or why Tobias was found at the Templar's building with his head bashed in. That remains a mystery at this present time. But I do know that the Masons, the Templars and the Illuminati now all have a copy of the Anthology in Latin. Oh, and Pastor Thaddeus has it memorized."

Holmes paused to draw in some smoke from his pipe and then exhaled a puff of smoke. A thin smile crossed my lips as his gaze met with mine. I knew this smile meant that Holmes had deliberately left out the fact that we also had a copy of part of the Secret Anthology.

"I hope I'm not going too fast for you, gentlemen," he said.

"But what good is this treasure map if it's in Latin?" Gregson asked.

"Good question, Inspector," Holmes answered. "But consider that everyone who has a copy is most probably well versed in Latin. So far the only ones who have had a go at it are Pastor Thaddeus and Mr. Merriweather. Neither of them was successful in figuring out the cipher. Now, we presume that we have several sets of fresh eyes scrutinizing it. Perhaps they will be successful, perhaps not. But one thing is certain. The odds for their success are certainly not in their favor, given that this secret has been well kept for centuries."

"Where does that leave us as far as our respective investigations?" Hopkins asked.

"Until we identify the second hooded man at the fire, he and the Secret Anthology are the keys to the case," Holmes said.

"Drat," Hopkins said.

Holmes smirked. "I'd use the death of Tobias to your advantage, Hopkins. Since Tobias was the prime suspect in the murder of Withermew, I suggest you convey this development to your Chief Constable. Mention that you are looking for further evidence to determine if he was indeed the culprit. He should be quite pleased that you have done so well in such a short time."

Hopkins seemed to be inflated by the advice.

"However," Holmes said. "I am not at all convinced that Tobias was the actual killer. From what we have gathered, he was purportedly trying to help Withermew protect the Secret Anthology. There was no reason for Tobias to kill him."

The inspector's countenance deflated immediately.

"I don't know how I'm going to solve this one," he said, his dejection obvious.

"Tut, tut, old boy," Holmes said. "Rest assured I will continue to pursue the investigation of this case and will see it through until it is solved. When we catch the actual killer, you will be in your Chief Constable's good graces."

Holmes took another long draw on his pipe stem and expelled some smoke out of the corner of his mouth. "That still leaves you with the murder of Chief Polk with which to contend. One thing that is clear is that Tobias is certainly absolved of that one because he wouldn't have gone to the trouble of dropping off the Secret Anthology for safe keeping with his best friend, and then subsequently murder him. That killing was most obviously perpetrated by someone else."

"But who?" Hopkins said.

"That we shall find out before this is over," Holmes said, rising from his perch and taking in a copious breath. "So there you have it, Inspectors three. You all, of course, are sworn to secrecy on the matter of the Secret Anthology and especially the silver crown. There is not to be a whisper of it until this case is solved." He paused to give each of them an emphatic stare. "You all are working on different facets of the same case. I've equipped you with the pertinent knowledge we have thus far." He paused and drew another heavy breath. "The three of you are the best that Scotland Yard has to offer. Use this information wisely."

"But—" Lestrade started to say.

Holmes cut the query off with a dismissive shake of his hand, and then flung his arm out and pointed towards the door. I was certain that there were questions on each of the Inspectors' minds, but his pose was like the statue of Apollo, frozen in granite, unmoving. The three men obviously knew they were being summarily dismissed and that any further talk would be useless. They gathered their hats, nodded their goodbyes to me, and departed. Holmes swung the door closed behind the last one.

"That should keep them out of our hair for the time being," he said.

"While we do what?" I asked.

He turned to me with an elevated eyebrow and a crafty smile. "Watson, we are going to concentrate on the Iron Crown today. If we can decode the part of the Secret Anthology and secure the relic, perhaps we can lure the mastermind behind all of this intrigue out into the open."

"What makes you think the killer will jump at the bait?"

He chuckled. "Oh, come now, old boy. It's painfully obvious."

"It is?"

"Certainly. It's the item that everyone is after. To the Masons, it's a symbol of prestige. If it were in their possession, they could display it as confirmation affirming that they are the world's oldest and most important fraternal organization." He drew on his pipe and expelled a vaporous cloud.

"And the Templars," he continued. "They want it for its value as a most holy relic. The nail from the True Cross of the Christ, to add it to the fabled collection of relics from the Holy Land they supposedly hold buried in England."

"And what of that other group?" I asked. "The Illuminati?"

Holmes removed the stem of the pipe from his mouth and when he spoke; his words were once again accompanied by a vaporous gray mist. "The Illuminati seek the Crown as a symbol of their far reaching power. Remember, it was used to coronate Holy Roman Emperors from Charlemagne to Napoleon. It's the oldest royal insignia in Christendom. What better icon for an organization that desires to rule the world to confer authority upon itself."

"And the Thieves' Guild?" I asked.

This query caused Holmes to elevate an eyebrow in consideration.

"An excellent question, old boy. Why indeed? But I would venture to speculate that like any good group of criminals, their motivation, and that of their leader, The Hawk, is most likely financial. The Iron Crown itself is of great monetary value alone, seeing that it's made up of precious metals and jewels, not to mention the high price any one of the three organizations, the Masons, the Templars, or the Illuminati, would pay for its safe return."

His brow furrowed and he cast a quick glance toward the door. A knock sounded moments later.

"Mr. Holmes?"

It was Mrs. Hudson's voice.

I strode to the door and opened it.

Out landlady stood there with a look of gestating exasperation on her face.

"There's another gentleman to see Mr. Holmes," she said.

"What?" Holmes said, striding over. "Who is it this time?"

"He's given the name Dr. Samuel Hester," she said.

Holmes and I exchanged glances.

"Thank you, Mrs. Hudson," Holmes said. "Do show him up."

Soon, Hester was at our door, greeting us both. "I'm sorry to call upon you without an appointment."

"Quite all right," Holmes said with a dismissive wave of his hand. "Do come in and have a seat."

"Oh, no," Dr. Hester said. "I shant be that long. I'm simply stopping by on behalf of Pastor Thaddeus."

"He's doing well, I hope?" Holmes asked.

The doctor frowned. "I'm afraid he's taken a turn for the worse. He was rather upset after your visit regarding the death of poor Randall."

"I'm sorry to hear that," Holmes said.

"Yes, as am I," Dr. Hester said. "But it couldn't be helped, I suppose. He retreated into a veritable fog after you left, babbling on and on, but today, when I visited him, I found him quite confused. But he did ask me whether or not you had made any progress on the case involving Randall Tobias' murder and the recovery of the Secret Anthology. I thought if I could offer him some news about the case, it might serve to comfort him."

"Unfortunately," Holmes said, "there is nothing of note to report on the murder of Mr. Tobias as yet. Except that we are sure that he wasn't killed there at the Templars, but somewhere else."

Dr. Hester's brow twitched. "And this Secret Anthology?"

"Well, as I told you, the original copy of the Secret Anthology is still residing with Scotland Yard, as far as I know." Holmes removed his pipe from his mouth and stroked his chin with his other hand. "You, of course, know that Polk sent a copy to the Templars, and I have now confirmed that the barrister, Langhorn, also had a copy, most likely obtained from Randall Tobias. And, of course, there's the one memorized by the good Pastor."

"Yes, of course." Dr. Hester nodded. "Well, the Pastor was wondering if you might have had the opportunity to see it while it was in police custody. With your powers of deduction, he thought that perhaps you might be able to shed some light on deciphering the riddle and locating the crown."

Holmes emitted a forced laugh. "I assure you, Dr. Hester, that the exploration of a dead language is not my forte. My appreciation of Latin died during my school days with Julius Caesar on the Ides of March."

"Mine as well." Dr. Hester chortled something akin to a laugh, and then his expression turned serious. "But Pastor Thaddeus and others have spent a lifetime trying to decipher the code to find the location of the Crown," he said. "He was hoping that you might lend your tremendous deductive reasoning skills to that task. It would mean a lot to him if he could go to his reward knowing the mystery was solved."

"I'm flattered by his estimation of my abilities." Holmes flashed a smile. "Tell the good man Inspector Hopkins was kind enough to copy down a page or two of the Anthology for me, and I have been examining it. Just out of curiosity, of course."

"Do you think you can decipher the riddle?" Dr. Hester asked. "As I told you, it would mean a lot to the Pastor."

"Tell him that I will take a look at it when I find time."

"Thank you. I shall convey this news to Pastor Thaddeus." Dr. Hester's mouth compressed into a thin line. "That will give the pastor some peace of mind. I shall take no more of your time, Mr. Holmes. He'll be most pleased."

We walked with him to the door.

"I bid you both good day, gentlemen," he said, and left.

I watched him descend the seventeen steps with what appeared to be a bit of alacrity. Mrs. Hudson closed the house door after him and glared up at me with exasperation. I smiled in return, hoping we'd not be burdened with any more intrusions this day.

"Mrs. Hudson is fit to be tied," I said.

"I don't doubt it," Holmes said.

"That Dr. Hester's a rather thoughtful chap, wouldn't you say, Holmes?"

"Yes, a rather concerned fellow," my companion replied. "A physician who's concerned for his patients. A credit to his profession, as are you."

With that he returned to the study and seated himself behind his desk once more. I went to my desk and began making entries in my medical journal, but out of the corner of my eye, I couldn't help but watch Holmes, wondering how he was going to make sense of all this. Pencil in hand, the detective spent the next two hours making countless drawings and calculations, getting frustrated with each one, and after a while, kept tossing them on the floor and starting over. The floor around him was littered with crumpled papers.

If Leonardo Da Vinci had used this method on the Mona Lisa, I remember thinking to myself, her smile would never have been completed.

He began drawing lines in the text books that he had purchased. Then he would leap from his chair and pace around the room, muttering to himself, his finger raised to his lips, until an idea apparently struck him. Then he would sit down once more at the desk and begin scribbling away.

The first interruption came approximately two hours or so later with another knock on the door. I rose and answered it, finding Mrs. Hudson standing there looking more frustrated than ever.

"Tell him that Inspector Lestrade is here again," she said in a subdued whisper. "And he says he needs to see Mr. Holmes immediately."

Before I could respond, I heard a resounding curse from the study.

My companion slammed his pencil down on the table and said in an irritated tone, "I will give him five minutes. Not a minute more."

Mrs. Hudson's mouth formed into an O shape and she quickly departed.

I turned to Holmes and cast him a stern look.

"You really should endeavor to be more courteous to her," I said.

"Yes, yes, yes," he said, running his fingers through his hair. "It's just that all these damn interruptions … What the Devil does he want now?"

Obviously hearing Holmes' rant, Lestrade entered gingerly. "Thank you for seeing me, Mr. Holmes. I know how busy you are."

"Yes, what is it, Inspector?" His tone was harsh.

"I just had a set-to with the Deputy Chief of Permits and Citations. He came into my office unannounced raving about how that Templar, the Duke Bouchard, had just left his office. They were screaming bloody hell about a reporter from the *Daily Telegraph* snooping around and asking questions about the body of that bloke that we found behind their building the other day."

"You mean poor Mr. Tobias?" I said.

"Yeah, that's the one." Lestrade compressed his lips for an instant. "Bouchard wants to know what in blazes we're doing about it, and when are we going to solve it. And to take the heat off the Templars, he wants it made known that the body was murdered someplace else and just dumped behind their building."

"I'm sure that you assured him Scotland Yard is working on the affair with all the diligence that they apply to all of their cases," Holmes said.

"I did," Lestrade said. "But a fat lot of good it did."

Holmes said nothing.

"Well," Lestrade continued. "In view of what you told us this morning, I was wondering if you had any further suggestions of what I might be saying?"

Holmes remained silent for several moments, and then a slight grin appeared on his face. "You might tell him, Inspector, that Mr. Tobias was murdered someplace else and was then dragged over to the Templars building. The only other viable alternative is that he walked over there, post mortem, to lie in repose."

Lestrade was not laughing. "I almost threw that Deputy Chief out of my office, the pompous ass. And who does that Bouchard think he is, sending a city hall official on Scotland Yard, like I answer to some glorified permit clerk with a fancy title. I've got better things to do with my time than to be bothered with irritating interruptions."

I was sure that the irony of Lestrade's words was lost on him.

"Here, here," Holmes said.

Lestrade sat there for several seconds, and when no one spoke further, a sheepish grin appeared on his face.

"Well, Mr. Holmes, you gave me some tips on how to handle that Bouchard fellow the last time. I thought perhaps you give'd me a few more now?"

"The tip I have for you, Lestrade," Holmes said, "is don't apply for any building permits in the next few weeks. Now, if you don't mind, I have some very important work here that I have to get back to. Good day,

Inspector." Holmes marched over to the door, opened it and motioned to the hallway. "Thank you for coming."

The Inspector walked quickly out of our room, head bowed. Holmes let the door swing shut behind him.

My friend walked briskly over to his desk, picked up one of the books on the Templars and then moved over to sit cross-legged in his usual chair by the fireplace. Within minutes, he was deep in thought, lost in that magnificent mind vault where he stored all the information that he considered pertinent to his profession.

His meditation lasted for over a half hour when Mrs. Hudson once again knocked on our door, jarring him out of his trance-like state.

"Dear God," his voice dripped in desperation. "How am I expected to get anything done with these constant interruptions? What is it, Mrs. Hudson?" he yelled.

I rose from my desk and went to the door.

"Inspector Hopkins to see you," she shouted back through the slightly opened door.

"Tell him that I'm out at the market buying melons for St. Swithen's Day," he shouted.

The Inspector popped his head around Mrs. Hudson, doffing his hat.

"Thank you, Mrs. Hudson," he said. "Sorry to drop in like this, Mr. Holmes, but I need your advice. It's about the murder of Mr. Tobias."

"That seems to be a very popular topic today," Holmes said sarcastically, getting up from his position that he had maintained for such a long time.

"I did as you suggested and passed on the conjecture that Tobias may be the killer of Dr. Withermew and Battalion Chief Polk," Hopkins said. "It satisfied my Chief Constable for a short time; but now he wants to know who killed Mr. Tobias? And I have no clue."

"Lestrade was just here with the same question," the detective said. "And I have no answer at the present time. I assure you that I am working on it, and giving the matter all of the attention it deserves. But there are also other pressing matters in this case that must be solved first that might help us answer that question."

"Do you have any suggestions as to what I might tell the Chief Constable, Mr. Holmes?" Hopkins was literally standing there with hat in hand.

"Tell him," Holmes paused. "Tell him that you are pursuing a viable lead concerning the man in the hood who was seen leaving the fire. He might be connected to the death of Tobias. He's as good a suspect as any at the present time."

"I shall do that," he said, his eyes widening.

"Hopkins," said Holmes."You're a reasonably bright fellow with adequate skills in lining up the facts and following them to a positive conclusion. Put your excellent deductive skills to full use and together we can solve this conundrum. Now, if you don't mind, I'm in the middle of my research and do not wish to be disturbed any further."

Hopkins expressed his gratitude and left. As the door closed, Holmes spun around and said, "Watson, get your revolver and stand guard at the door and shoot the next person who dares to try and enter."

"What if it's Mrs. Hudson with our dinner?" I said with a grin.

"*Especially*, if it is her," he replied.

Truth be told, I was getting ready to inquire about dinner when we were interrupted by three of Holmes' little urchins knocking urgently at the door having scampered up the stairs before Mrs. Hudson could corral them. I answered the door, and, right under my arm, they burst in, ran to my friend's side, and stood there at attention, ready to report.

"Mr. Holmes, we have a lot of news," the tallest one with the jacket whose sleeves were too short blurted out. "A lot of news."

"Oh, what is it, Wiggins?" Holmes asked, spinning in his chair to face the lad.

"There was a big fight between the Thieves' Guild and the Illuminates," the boy said. "Took place about a half hour ago. We saw it and then came right here."

"And what did you see?"

"It was real bloody," Wiggins said. "It started with them both planning things in two pubs."

The youth's words were coming so rapidly that he was practically breathless.

Holmes raised his hand, palm outward.

"Slow down, lad. First of all, it is the Illuminati, but let's refer to them as the lawyers instead. Now start at the beginning. What about them?"

The two young men looked at each other and then the one called Wiggins took a deep breath and began again. "Then that would be Bertie's turn. He was the one who hangs around the Blue Ale Pub."

Holmes turned his gaze upon the other young ruffian.

"Then you begin, Bertie," my companion said. "And do take your time."

"Well, Mr. Holmes." The urchin licked his lips. "I was listening to these men talking in the corner, about six or seven of them. And one says something about the Thieves' Guild. I knew you told us to look out for anything about that group, so I listened real good. They was talking about how their boss, The Hawk, told them to be going to some lawyer's house and killing him if he don't tell them what's what about the location of the crown."

It was then that Wiggins began coughing.

I went over and placed the back of my hand against the boy's forehead. It seemed hot, but not feverish.

"Seems you have the beginnings of a cold, young man," I said. "You should be in bed resting."

"Watson," Holmes said loudly. "Please get them some water. Go on, Bertie."

"That's when one of them took off his hat and he was the one. The one in the newspaper we was carrying with the scar on his head right here." Bertie's fingers traced the area over his left eyebrow.

"You are certain of this?" Holmes asked.

"Yes, sir, Mr. Holmes. He was the man all right. The man with the scar. That's when this fat man left the bar."

I returned with three glasses of water. Bertie paused in his recitation and gulped down the contents. He held it out, signifying that he wanted more. The other boys did the same. I took the glasses and went back to the water pitcher.

"And why is this fat man so important?" Holmes said raising his eyebrow.

"Because I seen him next," the third, and most diminutive of the trio, said. "A fat man."

I had seen this boy before out of our window. He was the one whose coat was a size too big for his small frame. He reminded me of a miniature scarecrow.

"I was at the Boar's Knob keeping an eye on the lawyer fellows like Wiggins told me to do. I was supposed to follow that Mr. Cording fellow like he asked. He was with a group of about two-times-ten men." He stopped and blushed. "I can't count past ten. I got real close to them, on account of me being so little, and they was talking about getting the men that jumped them the other day." The boy paused to wipe the elongated sleeve over his nose, which looked moist, and then drank from his glass.

"That's when I seen a fat man come running in. I seen he was Roller Swelly, one of the First Street Gang. Bertie told me later that was the same fat man that he'd seen earlier. The fat man was a spy. Bertie said he saw a man with a scar at the Blue Ale Pub. It was then that Wiggins comes in to check on me. The lawyer men left and we followed them. They took a bunch of carriages to the pub. Wiggins and me, we hitched a ride on the back of a brougham, real sneaky like."

"Well done, lads," the detective said, "what happened next?"

"The lawyer men went into the pub, the Blue Ale, and started throwing around chairs. The lawyer men had knives and two of them even had pistols. The Thieves' Guild guys had clubs and knifes, too. And they had some pistols as well. The men with the guns began shooting, so me and Bertie and Wiggins stayed outside and ducked for cover." He slurped down his second glass of water.

"There was shooting and hollering and things breaking," Wiggins jumped in. "When the shooting stopped I looked in the window and could see the men brawling mighty fierce. One cracked another one over the back with a chair and he fell down real hard. I saw another man get stabbed in the arm. Then one of them lawyers comes stumbling out the front door holding his stomach and falls dead right in front of us. We looked up and seen the thief man run out, the one with the scar. He got away. It was then that we figured it was time to get back here and tell you what we saw."

"An excellent job. Excellent. More water all around, Watson." Holmes walked over to his desk, opened the center drawer and withdrew a handful of coins. He stepped over to the still thirsty lads and started handing them several sovereigns each.

"You have outdone yourselves providing me with this information well before the best newspapers in London. Sleep well tonight knowing that you have performed a job well done."

With that he waved them towards the door. The looks on their smudged faces as they cradled their wages was of great satisfaction.

I, on the other hand, was not so satisfied.

"Holmes, how can you send those boys out to do your bidding and place them in the middle of a gun battle and put their lives in peril? Don't you think it's a bit unconscionable?"

"Oh, come now, Watson, they were never in any real danger. They were safely outside of the area of battle. They have the keen street acumen of the lower social class—the sense to keep low and avoid gunplay and knife fights. They are survivors, for heaven's sake. They live off their wits. And whatever I pay them."

"Or whatever they can steal," I said. "I'll bet Mrs. Hudson is none too happy with the caliber of visitors we've had today. Why, only one, that Hester fellow, showed any manners."

Holmes raised an eyebrow. "What's of more concern to me, Watson, is the escalation of the war between the three clandestine organizations and the Thieves' Guild has come sooner rather than later. I'm afraid our friends at Scotland Yard are going to have their hands full."

He spun around and sat, legs folded underneath him, back in his chair next to the table. "Now, if you don't mind, I'd like to turn my attention back to the cipher in the Secret Anthology once again. This Latin is giving me a headache."

"Maybe not eating and playing field marshal to your little troops has something to do with that."

Fortunately, there were no further interruptions for some time. Holmes spent the rest of the time reading another of the books that he had purchased, taking copious notes which he piled haphazardly around the table and floor. There were also now dozens of crumpled sheets lying about the room discarded by him. I had suggested to Mrs. Hudson a light supper of just sandwiches, hoping that Holmes would stop long enough to at least pick one up and eat it. But that was not to be as he was still engrossed in his Latin book and translations scattered about our room like an avalanche of snowflakes when she brought up the tray of food.

He barely looked at it.

I quietly ate but found little solace in the nourishment.

I feared that this complex riddle, replete with so much loss of life, was proving too much even for the greatest intellect I had ever known.

Time will tell, I thought, and indulged in some after-dinner smoking.

It was approximately an hour later when Holmes finally snapped the book shut, stood up, and stretched. I paused in my perusal of the evening paper and placed it down on my lap.

"This research is driving me crazy, Watson," he said. "The Free Masons are built on Medieval Guilds of stone masons, the first unions. The Illuminati were founded by power hungry aristocrats bent on secretly taking over the world. The Templars are a Catholic military order. And I can throw in Parliament as a bunch of inbred imbeciles. The whole world has gone insane."

I could see that the strain of trying to make sense of it all was having a detrimental effect on him, but there was little I could do.

Besides, I told myself. It's not like he hasn't been here before.

I repeated that out loud.

A thin smile graced his lips and he picked up his black clay pipe, the one he preferred when he was either concentrating or pontificating.

"Good old Watson," he said. "Always there to offer steadfast advice, be it medicinal or inspirational. Thank you, old chum."

"My pleasure. Now, perhaps if you would care to enlighten me a bit of what your vast amount of contemplative activity has brought to light …"

"Of course, old boy." He began packing some tobacco into the pipe. "This is how things are shaping up thus far. To understand meaning of the writing in the Secret Anthology one must not only have an understanding of the Latin inscriptions, but also be able to decipher a series of riddles."

"*Et tu*, Holmes?" I said with a smile.

He shot me a droll glance and set about lighting the tobacco in his pipe. Once he had it going, he continued.

"To be a Templar you had to profess that you believed in a Supreme Being," Holmes said. "But how would they know what you believed in your heart? I mean, one could say that I believed in fairies and pixies and you wouldn't know if I truly meant it."

"Holmes, are you belittling fairies and pixies?" I said, trying to maintain a bit of levity in the conversation. "Or do you really believe in them?"

He chuckled. "My dear Watson, that is no more far-fetched than believing in the stories that you spin for *The Strand*."

I had to smile at that one. I was further delighted with the direction that the conversation had now taken. My friend seemed to have completely shaken the tenebrous mood that had been plaguing him earlier.

"Did you know," he continued. "That the Templars invented banking as we know it today?"

"Yes. I do believe you mentioned that before."

"They amassed a fortune in gold and land. They even once owned the entire island of Cyprus. Kings and Queens of every country came to borrow money from them to finance their wars and expeditions. And you said history was boring."

"I said no such thing," I protested.

"On their crusades to the Holy Land they acquired many holy relics. Their headquarters was in the Temple of Solomon in Jerusalem and that will prove important, I dare say. It is said they once possessed the Ark of the Covenant, the Holy Grail, pieces of the True Cross and, of course, the nails from that cross. Legend has it that they returned to France, Italy and England with these treasures."

"If they were so rich and powerful, what happened to them?" I asked.

"King Philip IV of France and King Edward II of England happened." He blew out a plume of smoke. "King Philip was deeply in debt to the

Templars and Edward wanted to get the Earl of Cornwall out of exile, so he went along with Philip and declared the Templars heretics and defilers of the cross. All trumped up charges mind you, and on October thirteen, 1307 had them all rounded up and imprisoned. Of course, their wealth and lands were confiscated."

"Of course," I said.

"Some people attribute the superstition of Friday the thirteenth arising from that event."

"Remarkable," I said. I was so engrossed in Holmes tale that I had let the newspaper slip from my hands and fall to the floor. As I bent to pick it up the thoughts of the pageantry and drama danced through my imagination. Then a stray thought slipped in, like a piece of paper that has been suddenly thrust underneath a closed door. Would Holmes retain this fascinating information or would he discard it as not useful when the case was solved? My guess was he would file it somewhere within that remarkable mind of his, subject to recalling it at a moment's notice should the situation arise in which he needed it.

"But here is what struck me as strange," he said, as if offering a clue to my unasked mental query. "The Templars headquarters was the Temple Mount in Jerusalem, otherwise known as the Ruins of the Temple of Solomon. They were, in fact, once known as the Order of Solomon's Temple, which became shortened to the Templars." He paused to draw upon the pipe once more.

"The word 'temple' comes up in the Latin text in the Secret Anthology very prominently," he said. "*Temple*, Watson. That is the key. Their *Temple* Mount. Our *Temple* Hill. Temple. Are you up for a trip to the Temple Hill District tomorrow?

"Certainly, Holmes. Fresh country air will do us some good. But I suspect we are not going there to relax."

He blew out another great plume of smoke and smiled. "You know me too well, old friend."

"King Phillip was deeply in debt to the Templars..."

CHAPTER 13

MIDNIGHT IN THE GRAVEYARD

It was eight o'clock Saturday morning when I walked into our sitting room and found Holmes already eating toast and jam with his hard-boiled egg. Another plate sat on the table across the way, a cloth napkin resting on top. He was still surrounded by the pile of books.

"Good morning, Watson. I hope that you don't mind that I had Mrs. Hudson bring breakfast up early." He gestured to the other plate.

"I'm just glad that you're consenting to take in a bit of sustenance," I said.

"Quite right, old boy. I did find myself in need of something after having labored virtually all night."

I sat down and removed the napkin from my plate. One partially eaten hardboiled egg sat on the dish along with a few errant crumbs and nothing else. Holmes had evidently eaten not only his toast, but mine as well.

Before I could offer any protestations he laughed.

"Don't fret, Watson. I've already sent word downstairs and Mrs. Hudson is now preparing you a regal feast, fit for a king. She should be bringing it up shortly."

I frowned a bit and picked up the pitcher to pour myself a spot of tea while I waited, but that pot was empty as well.

"Great Scott," I said. "You've not only recovered your appetite, but usurped mine as well."

Holmes roared with laughter, which I took as a good sign. It did me good to see my friend so ebullient.

"I thought we'd get a fresh start on our journey to Lincolnshire," he said. "The Temple Hill District, to be more exact. And, you're absolutely correct. The time spent the last few days going over all those books on Templar lore and Mason symbols has given me a tremendous appetite. Upon sating my hunger, optimism returned to me. I'm totally convinced that my review of that Latin tome will bear fruit today. Perhaps we will uncover the first clue and that will, in turn, lead us to the next clue, if it exists. I do believe that I have extrapolated the location indicated by the first verse of the Secret Anthology."

As he said that there came the familiar knocking on the door and

Holmes sprang to his feet and rushed to answer it.

He opened it and said, "Ah, Mrs. Hudson, as Dr. Watson always says, you're a vision of loveliness, just like an angel bringing much needed sustenance at the emergence of the new day."

The old girl smiled and I thought she almost had to stifle a giggle. She beamed as she brought the tray over to the table and set it down in front of me, evidently taken in by his rakish charm.

Perhaps she won't be raising the rent after all, I thought.

When I'd finished my breakfast, I packed and made sure that I put my service revolver in my Gladstone. We were off by carriage in no time. Soon we caught the nine-thirty train out of the Charing Cross station and settled in our coach. We were fortunate enough to get a compartment all to ourselves. At noon, we ate the sandwiches which Mrs. Hudson so thoughtfully packed for us and settled in for our several hour-long trip north. We relaxed to the rhythm of the swaying train.

"Holmes, what exactly did you learn from all your reading yesterday?"

He shifted his weight to pull a crumpled piece of paper out of his jacket pocket.

"We're searching for the Iron Crown taken by the Templars and brought to England, its location marked by the coded Anthology. I finally isolated the key lines that pointed to the location of the first clue. It was the Latin verse, *Ad seplulorum in statu gravis templum collis*. But I must say, Watson, your handwriting here is atrocious. It's bad enough that the Latin they wrote it in is not classical, but a sloppy mixture of ancient Greek and Old English. I had to go through many, many translations on every line until it made sense."

"Well," I said indignantly. "I will certainly speak to those dead Templars who wrote it the next time I see them."

"Be that as it may, it roughly translates as, 'The grave in a serious state in a temple on or off the hill.' But working on the end of the sentence it can also be translated as 'in serious state on a temple hill.' That was the key."

"How so?" I asked.

He frowned, as if explaining the solution of a complex equation to a simpleton, and sighed. "I worked the sentence over and over again, and then it suddenly became clearer to me. The Templars' headquarters was the Temple Mount in Jerusalem. The temple on the hill. Temple Hill."

Holmes was now facing me, very animated.

"The second line reads, '*Magister confractus vultus gravi.*' It was the word *magister* that confused me. It means master." He held up an extended index finger. "Until I realized that it could also be translated as the Mediaeval word '*praecptoria*,' or preceptor. The head master. And since the rest of the sentence is 'faces a serious cross break,' it came to me that '*gravis*' can also be a 'grave'; which can be translated as 'head stone.'"

I was completely baffled by his explanation.

Holmes clapped his hands. There was a joyful grin across his lips, as if he were a school boy who just figured out the Pythagorean Theorem.

He must have sensed my befuddlement for he frowned slightly and continued.

"And where, pray tell, does a *preceptor* hold sway?" He waited a few beats, and then said, "In a preceptory of course. A stronghold built by Templars to shelter travelers and to raise money and recruit soldiers. I found such a preceptory right there in Temple Hill. It was a monastery of military order under the command of the Knights Templars. Like all proper preceptories, it has a round nave on its church copied from the Holy Sepulchre in Jerusalem, built on the banks of a river with a graveyard on its southern exposure. There we shall find our graveyard and headstone."

"Absolutely brilliant, Holmes," I said. "You've figured out the first clue."

"Ah, Watson, if it so, then we shall hope to find the second clue there also."

He rubbed his hands together. That far away look drifted over his eyes as he retreated into that contemplative state where he would take pleasure in ruminating on a conundrum in the silence that he so often craved.

I slowly nodded off with a smile on my lips and visions of knights and crusades filling my dreams.

In a couple of hours we arrived at North Wickham in Lincolnshire. There we leased a trap, a relatively new buggy at that, and threw our luggage in the back. I took the reins and drove down a pleasant country lane to an inn to which the station master had given us directions. We took two rooms at the small, charming inn with a thatched roof and sat down to a meal of porridge. After dinner, the innkeeper gave us directions to the preceptory.

The sun was working its way down in the western sky and the cooler night air was causing the fog to creep slowly along the ground. Holmes insisted that we set off now, saying that we could reconnoiter the graveyard tonight and go back tomorrow. His excitement was causing him to look as if he were going to burst at his seams. We secured two lanterns from the innkeeper and set out for the preceptory at a slow trot. It was less than ten minutes until we arrived at the pond in front of the ruins of the ancient church. There, at the south end of the structure, was a good sized grave-yard. We set the hand brake, tied the reins of our horse to the withered husk of a fallen tree, and lighted our lanterns as the sun had just dropped below the horizon. The fog had now enveloped the countryside as thick as any that filled the streets of London.

We carefully made our way through the wet grass among the grave-stones and markers, some toppled, others teetering precariously, while others were majestically upright, very ornate with angels and carved vases and crosses adorning their tops. The fog and the glow of our lanterns gave the scene a gloomy, spectral atmosphere.

"What exactly are we looking for, Holmes?"

"A grave in a serious state, Watson. We are looking for a tomb of some-one important that is in a state of disrepair, long battered by the elements, with a serious cross break. A broken cross on it."

A few seconds later, Holmes stumbled over a piece of a broken head-stone buried in the tall grass.

"Do be careful," I called out. "It's treacherous out here."

"Yes," he called back, "just keep an eye out for an important grave."

The fog was a thick as pea soup. It clung to the ground and actually seemed to be affixed to my trouser legs. Both Holmes and I began to tap the ground ahead of ourselves with our walking sticks to alert ourselves to any loose stones or tangled underbrush.

"Ah-ha," Holmes cried out, "I think I've found it, Watson."

I could barely make out where he was in the eerie grey landscape. Slowly the glow of his lantern came into view and I made my way to his side. He was standing beside a large square mausoleum. Its surface was well worn and chipped. A top corner had been knocked off. It was, indeed, in a serious state.

"It is the tomb of a very important master or preceptor. It says 'Preceptoria Sir Edmund Sinclair of High Wycolmbe.' He reached out and touched the mausoleum as if to verify it was really standing there in front of him and not an apparition in the evening fog.

"Look at the inscription on this side, Watson," he said holding his lan-tern up to illuminate the carved letters. "It translates 'in this sign thou shall conquer.' And above it is carved a Templars' cross but purposely broken in the middle by a large slash carved across it. We have found our serious cross break."

He rubbed his gloved hand over the inscription.

"Now, is there a second clue to be had?" he murmured.

He held his lantern aloft and began to circle the tomb. I followed him around the crypt.

"There's a Latin inscription on this side," he said. "But it is worn from years of the weather. Watson, do you have your note book with you?"

"Surely, Holmes, I have it right here in my coat pocket." I reached in and withdrew my pencil and book.

He again rubbed his hand over the letters, brushing away ages of dirt and held his lantern near to the inscription." This is practically indecipherable," he said. "But I shall try."

He leaned closer and stared at the inscription with intensity.

"It translates, 'In the center of the kingdom, the king without a crown will point to the greatest sign under God's eye. In this sign thou shall conquer.'"

He held his lantern closer and read the inscription again, this time whispering the Latin and then his translation to himself. "That's the best I can do. Some of the letters are completely worn off." He huffed and lowered his lantern.

It was then that I noticed a faint glow off in the distance coming towards us. Its ethereal glow seemed to illuminate several ghostly forms.

"Holmes," I whispered. "It appears that we're not alone."

"No," he said, looking at the approaching men. "It does not."

The shadowy group suddenly split apart as the large glow became two separate ones.

"It looks like there are four of them," I said, *sotto voce*. "But I can barely make them out. Who are they?"

"They must have followed us from the inn," he whispered. "Quick, turn your lantern down. Wait to see if they call out. Let's see what their intentions might be."

"Whom do you think they might be?" I asked. "And how in the Devil did they know we were here?"

"That is something we must endeavor to find out, old boy," he said. "But first things first. Let's worry about staying out of harm's way, shall we?"

"But of course," I said, reaching into my pocket to feel the reassurance of my Webley revolver.

I dosed the flame of my lantern, kept my eyes on the two separate groups of figures as they stumbled around in the fog. I withdrew my pistol from my coat pocket.

"Oww," one cried out. "Damn this fog."

"Quiet, you fool," another said. "I think they're right up ahead."

"I didn't know I'd be stumbling around in a graveyard when I agreed with this," a third voice chimed in.

"The Hawk will have our heads if we don't find out what these two found out here in the country," said the first man.

The Hawk again, I thought. We were being stalked by an unknown adversary with far reaching and sinister tentacles. He'd obviously had us followed from London.

"Shut yer damn mouth," the second one admonished. "Look. I don't see their light no more."

Like ghosts out of a Dickens novel, the phantoms kept approaching, now shuffling their feet to keep their balance. Their lanterns swayed to and fro, appearing to be floating apparitions in the thick fog.

Out of the haze two ruffians appeared about fifteen feet from Holmes. I could barely make out that the one closest to him had a club in his left hand. Suddenly, the detective sprang up and brought his cane down hard on the thug's wrist. The man cried out in pain and I immediately wondered if the blow had broken the bone. The weapon fell to the ground as the assassin continued to howl in pain. Holmes quickly swung his stick back in an upward motion and forcefully chopped at the chest of the second man who held the lantern. The breath escaped from his body as the lantern dropped from his grasp.

This ruffian was a bigger man and the blow only stunned him for a second. He quickly sprang forward and rushed my companion, head down. The force of the collision bowled Holmes back into a small grave marker that tumbled over with both of them on top of it. The thug landed right next to the cudgel and grabbed the billy club from the wet grass as he regained his footing. Holmes sprang to his feet and held out his cane with both hands. As the assailant made a looping overhand thrust the detective blocked it, using his skill in single stick fighting.

Holmes jabbed the big man in the stomach with the brass head of his cane, doubling the thug over. The detective then deftly slammed his stick forcefully down on the man's shoulder. The stunned assailant dropped down to one knee. As the thug looked up, Holmes twisted his body, drew his cane back, and swung it with two hands across the head of the ruffian.

I heard a cracking sound as the brute slumped to the ground. Next to him lay the first ruffian still holding his wrist and howling in pain. Holmes pointed his walking stick into the chest of the whimpering, hobbled man, "Don't even think about moving."

This fracas did not go unnoticed by the second pair of thugs who were approximately ten feet to my right, and still around fifteen feet from my position. I stepped out from behind the cover of the mausoleum brandishing my revolver and got the drop on them.

"Halt," I shouted. "One move and you'll be shot."

To emphasize my resolve, I cocked back the hammer of the Webley.

They surrendered meekly. I bound the captives securely with their belts while Holmes kept watch with my pistol. Of the other two, one was still unconscious and the second one was wincing in pain. They weren't going anywhere.

"I recognize this fellow with the broken wrist from my criminal index, Watson. You'll find him under 'D.' Dubbins is his name, I believe."

"Dullard would seem more appropriate," I said.

Holmes smiled. "Yes, quite. Dubbins is a bone crusher and a collection man. He's also purported to be a pretty good tracker and surveillance man. No doubt that's how he kept out of our notice on our way up here."

"I wonder who they're working for?" I asked.

"I overheard them mention someone," Holmes said, "but not by name. Indeed, someone has recruited the services of the underworld to act as their agents. But it will do them no good in the long run."

"It seldom does," I said, "when they cross paths with the greatest detective of all."

Holmes brushed off my compliment with a shrug. He then turned to the howling man.

"I say," Holmes said. "It appears as if you may have a severe fracture, old boy. I could have my associate take a look. He is an exceptional doctor, you know."

The man stopped moaning long enough to snarl a profane response.

"It seems my attempt at referral to your medical practice has fallen short," Holmes said.

"I'm sure my practice will survive," I said.

"And how about you, Dubbins?"

One of the men's head pricked up, but he said nothing.

"Yes," Holmes continued. "I recognize you. Now do make it easier on yourself and tell us who employed you four to accost us."

This elicited another vulgar epithet similar to the other thug's utterance.

Holmes had an expression of amusement on his face as he turned back to me.

"It seems the vocabulary of these four is as limited as their intellects," he said.

"Quite," I replied.

Holmes then addressed the group. "I'll wager the four of you are here at the behest of a scoundrel known as The Hawk, who promised you a substantial reward, should you intercept us in our mission. He must have inferred that we were looking for something very valuable."

None of the four spoke.

Holmes sighed and turned to me.

"Obviously, they fear the retribution of this Hawk fellow more than us," he said.

I nodded, knowing he was right. Although we'd surely bested them in the confrontation, the ruffians knew that we were gentlemen, bound by a code of honor, whereas this Hawk fellow was obviously not.

"But it is also a good reminder," Holmes said in a loud voice, "that sending a quartet of buffoons seldom achieves any success. I pray you'll relay that message to him upon your return to London."

I moved forward and checked the injured man's wrist and found it wasn't a fracture, but instead a very severe sprain. I told him he should keep it immobilized for the present.

He grunted something resembling a thanks.

"Good old Watson," Holmes said. "Still bound by his Hippocratic oath."

With that, Holmes stepped over and grabbed their two lanterns, extinguishing both.

"I'd advise you not to go crawling around here without any lighting," Holmes said. "It could be hazardous to your well being."

"You can't just leave us here," one of them cried out. "It ain't decent."

"As if you had any thoughts of decency when you came stalking us with cudgels," I said.

That seemed to quiet them.

"Fear not, gentlemen," Holmes said in a good natured tone. "It should be dawn in several hours, and hopefully the sun will burn off some of this dreadful fog so you'll be able to find your way back. Now we must be on our way. I wish you gentlemen a pleasant evening."

Their pleas and moans continued as we began to carefully make our way back through the maze of broken tombstones.

"When you do get back," Holmes called out. "You can tell your employer that your trip here was a waste of time."

With that we left them there in the blanket of fog and made our way to our carriage. Next to it we found a hay wagon, obviously the mode of transportation of our attackers.

"I'm still wondering who sent them after us?" I said.

"It could be any number of suspects. Eventually, the answer will reveal itself, but in the meantime, we have much to do." He stopped to stroke the snout of the horse harnessed to the hay wagon. "I couldn't bear the thought of this poor beast being left unattended all night."

"Heaven forbid," I said with a knowing smile. It would have been foolish to leave a mode of quick transportation standing by, in case the four assailants somehow managed to free themselves and complete the arduous trek through the darkened cemetery.

Holmes elected to drive the wagon back to the inn while I drove our trap knowing that the four ruffians would have a hefty hike back, come daybreak.

CHAPTER 14

HOLMES AND THE THIEVES' GUILD

Early Sunday morning we were up at the break of dawn and had a hearty breakfast at the inn. There was still no sign of the four men who attacked us. We packed our bags and then threw them into our trap and rode to the station to catch the early train back to London. I tried to stretch my shoulder and leg to get the kinks out from the dampness they had endured the previous night. Holmes spent most of the time studying my notations of the inscription of the Latin verses on the mausoleum. He filled the pages of my tiny notebook up until there were none left. Eventually, I drifted off to sleep for the remainder of the journey. We arrived at Charing Cross a little after twelve-thirty and from there made our way back to Baker Street. Before entering our flat, Holmes stopped at Dawe's Book Shop and purchased a map and two books on landmarks of London.

When we arrived next door at our apartment there was Wiggins, the young, thin street urchin, standing next to the stoop. When he saw us, he began to fidget with excitement. He ran to the side of my companion and tugged on his coat.

"Mr. Holmes. I've got some more information for you. It's about the Thieves' Guild."

"Well, let's have it, Wiggins. Your information is always most welcome," the detective said bending down slightly.

"I've heard that fellow called The Hawk's real interested in that silver crown. The boys say that he's got his men hanging around pubs listening for any information they can get. I think they want to steal it."

"Quite right, Wiggins," Holmes said, frowning a bit. "But this is hardly enlightening."

The boy's face twitched with a look of desperation and I couldn't help but wonder when the last time was that he'd had a decent meal. I shuddered thinking about the poor lad's lot in life, always scrounging for a living.

"But wait, sir," Wiggins said, desperation edging into his tone. "I think the bloke with the scar's at the Blue Ale Pub where they had that fight the other night."

Holmes smiled. "Now that is a very useful bit of information. That is very good, indeed." He reached into his pocket and pulled out a sovereign, handed it to the lad, and tousled the boy's head. "This is for a job well done. Now be off with you and keep your ears to the pavement."

Wiggins scampered off down the street as if Christmas had come early.

"Poor wretch," I muttered.

"Quite," Holmes said, also looking at the boy's fleeing form. "But such is his lot. There's little we can do to change the way of the world, old boy."

I joined my friend on the steps. "And how is what he told you good news, Holmes?"

"If all goes well, we may be able to catch the killer of Mr. Langhorn for Inspector Gregson this evening. That is if you don't mind accompanying me out for a few pints tonight?" There was a twinkle in his eye.

"Of course not. There is nothing else I'd rather do. But why do I suspect that this will involve more than a simple drink or two?"

Holmes laughed. "Oh, Watson, you do know me too well."

Mrs. Hudson seemed relieved to see us, making me believe that Holmes' last round of compliments had put us squarely in her good graces. "I have a letter for you, Mr. Holmes. I'll fetch it and bring it right up to you."

"We'd be most grateful," he said. "You're a rare jewel, my dear."

She bustled off with a jaunty step and I leaned closer to him and whispered, "Laying it on a bit thick, aren't you, old boy?"

"On the contrary," he said, ascending the stairs one step ahead of me. "I'm merely hedging my bets for the next round of distemper that is surely to come sooner rather than later."

When we got to our quarters, we had just settled into our usual chairs when Mrs. Hudson knocked on the door and entered with the letter for Holmes. My friend once again thanked her profusely, and she departed, still in the grip of his good mood.

"Ah, Watson, this could be the letter I was waiting for." He tore the envelope open and quickly read its contents. "Yes, it is as I suspected. At last, I may have all the information that I need to put the final pieces of the puzzle together."

"What is it?" I inquired.

"It's too early to make a final pronouncement, but I shall have this solved by morning for sure. Perhaps I should inform the rest of the fellows of tomorrow's plans. He sat at the desk and wrote four separate messages. He counted out change from his desk drawer and went down the stairs. Once outside, he flagged down a messenger on bicycle and handed him the notes and the coins.

Upon returning upstairs, he had a sly grin on his face. "That should complete today's tasks. Now, Watson, I have someone I need to visit this afternoon. I won't be requiring your assistance. You can amuse yourself with your own tasks while I am gone. I shall not be that long."

"I've plenty to do," I said. "Including starting to write up the account of this adventure."

Holmes started to address me, but then hesitated.

"Whatever," he said. "Until later."

With that, he picked up his hat and cane and was out the door.

A vestige of curiosity regarding his sudden reticence perplexed me, but having been long familiar with the detective's eccentricities, I didn't let it bother me. I had no real plans made so I spent the remainder of the morning in reading the early edition newspapers. I had a mid-afternoon snack as Mrs. Hudson made small cucumber sandwiches for me and for Holmes in case he came back. And since he didn't, and I couldn't let her efforts go unappreciated. I nibbled on the other ones, and soon there was none.

It was a quarter to five when Holmes arrived back at Baker Street. I found myself paging through the evening papers when I heard the sound of his familiar voice bellowing a hearty acknowledgement to Mrs. Hudson.

"I fixed you some cucumber sandwiches," I heard her say.

"How sweet of you," Holmes said, his voice carrying through the closed door. "But I'll wager that Dr. Watson's voracious appetite has already seen to their consumption."

He burst through the door, filled with energy, his voice crackling with vitality.

"Hurry, Watson, we must get prepared to go out tonight. But first, I require a slight wardrobe adjustment."

"And just where might we be going?"

"To hoist a few," he said, mimicking the vernacular of the lower social class. "To stalk our quarry. And I'd best give you a slight modification from your usual sartorial elegance."

"My what?"

With that, there was a flourish of activity in our sitting room. The next half hour was spent in Holmes closet trying on various jackets. I wasn't sure if we were going out drinking or going to a costume ball. When we were finally deemed what he felt was appropriately dressed, we left for our destination on the lower North End of London in an area trying to make a comeback from being a poorer section of the city back to respectability.

At approximately quarter to six, we flagged down a cab.

After we'd settled in the coach, the slot above us opened and the driver asked where we were bound.

"The Blue Ale Pub," Holmes said. "On the North End."

The man's face lit up when he saw the amount, but then his brow furrowed.

"I say, gents," he said. "Are you sure two fine gentlemen like yourselves want to be going in that place? I must tell you, there were some foul dealings done there recently."

"The murder of Llewellyn Langhorn the previous Wednesday evening," Holmes replied. "Why else would we be going there?"

"Suit yourselves then," the driver grunted and slammed the slot closed.

We arrived in the same brougham, but alighted several blocks away from the establishment.

"It's imperative that we arrive separately, Watson," he said. "You go first, and I'll follow."

I was dressed in a pea coat and sailor's knit cap, giving my best impersonation of a seaman, all the while cradling my trusty service revolver in my pocket. Holmes was in a riding jacket and high boots, with a bushy moustache and unkempt eyebrows to match, carrying a riding crop. I entered the pub and slipped over to the corner to secure a small table by myself. A few minutes or so later my friend came in and stood over by the bar.

The Blue Ale Pub wasn't what one would call the finest drinking establishment in London. In fact, it was a tavern whose best days were long past. Its interior was dated but clean and still well appointed and served beer and spirits at a reasonable price, giving it a loyal following of professionals and working class men.

Instead of blending into the shadows as I had done, Holmes did his best to stand out, being boisterous and slurring his words, as if he had already had one pint too many. He began regaling anyone who would listen with a tale about an ancient silver crown of the realm that was recently discovered after being hidden for years and was worth a king's ransom. He called it the Crusader's crown and said he and his comrades had come about it in the ruins of an old church in Blackmoor. He bemoaned the fact that his unscrupulous partners had cheated him out of his share of the prize, but swore that he was going to seek them out tonight and confront them where they were settled with the treasure and reclaim his rightful share. After ordering another pint of ale, most of which he managed to spill on himself or on the floor, he pushed himself away from the bar and stumbled to the door.

Before I could get up, a young lanky fellow left from the far corner of the bar, with his bowler cocked back on his head, and trailed Holmes outside. Three other men quickly followed. A few seconds later I followed, hands in my pockets and head down as nonchalantly as possible.

Once outside I took note of Holmes who was weaving down the walkway, brushing against the lamppost, and continuing on his way with an unsteady gait. His staggering steps were like a pendulum on a hallway clock. It was then that I spotted two young toughs and an older dark haired man following him about twenty paces behind. I saw that the older man was brandishing a small club. Then the lanky young one pulled a knife from his pocket. My first instinct was to rush to the aid of my friend, but Holmes had instructed me to wait for his signal before engaging any assailants in our evening's travails. I did quicken my step to close the distance between myself and the menacing group.

"Hey, you bugger," the one with the knife called out. "We gotta talk with you."

Holmes spun around slowly and teetered.

"What can I do for you lads?" he slurred.

"We heard you spouting off about a silver crown back in the pub."

"The Crusader's crown," Holmes corrected him. "And what of it?"

His affected Cockney accent was perfect.

"We'd like to talk to you about it, too." the older man said. They began to circle him. The one with the club now began to smack it menacingly into the palm of his hand. The unarmed one just stood by Holmes' side and cracked his knuckles.

"Nah," Holmes said, the words dripping out of his mouth with exaggerated slowness. "I'm too busy to talk with you now. I've got to see some rotten scoundrels about my fair share."

"You'll talk with us first, you old sot." The tall thief now flashed his knife in front of Holmes and waggled it back and forth. "We got some business, eh? Now, you be real nice and tell us what we want to know, and we might let you live."

"I'd certainly like to live, you young pup," Holmes sputtered. "But you don't scare me. I'll have you know that I was a Captain in the Light Dragoons. Best damn horseman in the entire regiment."

"You ain't got no horse now, gov'ner," one of the other toughs said. "So let's talk some about this crown you are going to go get."

The thug with the knife moved closer.

"Well, halloo," Holmes shouted.

That was the signal. As I rushed forward, I drew my pistol from my pocket. Holmes, meanwhile, raised his riding crop and, with a wicked downward motion, slashed at the young thief's wrist, opening a gash and causing him to drop his knife. Holmes then spun around and whipped the older thug holding the billy club across the face. A crease opened on the man's cheek gushing out a splash of blood. The hooligan dropped the club and grabbed his wound, trying to stop the blood that was now flowing down his neck. The third tough stood there momentarily stunned. Holmes reached out, grabbing the ruffian's face and pushed his head back hard into the brick wall behind him. There was a loud crack and he slumped like a sack of potatoes to the ground.

"Hold it right there," I yelled breathlessly as I arrived brandishing my revolver.

"Well done, Watson." Holmes grinned. "Johnny on the spot, as usual."

I gazed down at the fallen trio.

"Not that I was needed," I muttered.

"Nonsense, old boy," Holmes said, clapping me on the shoulder. "Your arrival was as timely as that of the Light Brigade."

I frowned at the analogy. "And about as useful."

"Tut, tut. Though I must say I had the element of surprise on my side. They hardly expected that much fight out of an old drunkard. You know, I have always preferred the riding crop to the cane as an offensive weapon. Much more versatile." He snapped it along the side of his leg.

"And effective," I added.

"Look who we have here?" Holmes said with a smile looking down at the older thug lying prone on the pavement holding his bleeding face. "Our man with the scar above his left eye. It looks like now he'll have a matching one on his right cheek. Inspector Gregson will be happy to see him and his fellows."

"Will they now?" I said.

"Indubitably," he said. "These three are part of the Thieves' Guild and are responsible for the murders of Longhorn and the other barristers."

"Who are you?" one of the toughs asked. "You with the police?"

"We'll be asking the questions, if you don't mind," I said. "Now, where might we find The Hawk?"

The man spat a vulgar, guttural response.

I stiffened at the insult. Holmes placed a calming hand on my arm.

"Don't trouble yourself, old boy," he said. "We'll leave these scoundrels to authorities. I have all the answers I require to bring this case to its conclusion."

"You do?" I asked.

"Most certainly." There was a contented look on Holmes' face. His eyes were sharply focused on the three captives and a slight smile crept across his lips. "Now if you'd be so kind as to blow the whistle that you brought with you, perhaps we can get some constables here to clean up this mess and head home."

Two constables arrived shortly. We explained the situation, the hardest part being convincing them that we were indeed Sherlock Holmes and Dr. Watson. Finally, Holmes peeled off the hirsute elements of his facial disguise and they were then convinced. We delivered the three members of the Thieves' Guild to them with our regards to Inspector Gregson.

We were both still flushed with excitement when we arrived back at Baker Street. A glass of sherry calmed us down a little and we said goodnight to each other, knowing that we did a fair night's work.

"Now, where might we find the Hawk?"

Chapter 15
Elementary

It was a bright, sunny Monday morning and Baker Street was bustling with activity below us as Mrs. Hudson cleared away the breakfast dishes. I settled in my chair and unfolded the morning *Daily Telegraph* to catch up on the news of London. Holmes had already replaced the dishes with several books and more sheets of the papers that he had worked on yesterday.

Not a word was spoken between us until about quarter of nine when Holmes blurted out something akin to a groan.

"Having a bit of indigestion?" I asked.

He shook his head.

"There is one phrase that stands out, Watson, that keeps repeating itself." He leaned back and recited, 'In this sign thou shall conquer.' It's very clear to me that the meaning is significant, yet cloaked in mystery and misdirection. I just hope that John Randolph Secret wasn't suffering from the ravages of old age and just repeating himself or he was doubling up his phrases for emphasis. But I am beginning to suspect that he is referring to the sign of the cross."

He then carried on in silence for about two hours, when once again, the quietness was broken.

"Where the Devil is that piece of paper upon which I wrote that translation yesterday?" he exclaimed. "It has to be around here someplace."

He dropped to the floor, sat cross legged, and began tossing the scattered pages up in the air, letting them fall where they may, in search of that one particular sheet. Papers fluttered down like so many white flakes from the London sky covering the floor like a patchwork of winter snow.

"Ah, here it is," he exclaimed. Then all went quiet again.

An hour later he emitted another enunciated grunt.

"See right here, old fellow, the center is not a reference to the words but to a geographical place." Then he fell silent once more.

He ignored lunch and kept working. About an hour more had passed by when, with the book on landmarks laid out before him and his magnifier in his hand, he whispered, "Ha, it is west."

Again, the pall of stillness fell across the room like a black drape being drawn across a window.

I had no trouble concentrating on the rest of the *Telegraph* as it was now quiet for the rest of the afternoon. Mrs. Hudson had just set the dinner on the table and I had started in on the meal alone when after perhaps ten minutes Holmes spun around in his chair and announced, "I think I'll join you, Doctor. It's been a very successful afternoon. The answer to the puzzle is now fairly clear in my mind."

The suddenness of this pronouncement took me by surprise. Holmes had finished his elucidation and was joining me for dinner? It was truly an unexpected turn of events.

"Well," I said. "What did you find out?"

"All in good time, my friend." He seated himself in the chair opposite me, unfolded his napkin, and picked up his knife and fork. "But now, let's eat quickly because there's a concert that we should take in tonight at the Royal Albert Hall."

"A concert?" said I.

"It's a tribute to Karol Lipinski," he said. "His music rivaled that of Paganini. In fact, Paganini dedicated a work to him. Lipinski's Stradivarius compositions are sublime. If the orchestra comes even close to capturing his angelic sound then we are in for a memorable evening. We deserve to indulge ourselves." He smacked his fingers to his lips. "What say you, Watson?" He had a devious grin twisting across his face.

"I say that if you have everything well in hand, then we should certainly take an evening off to enjoy the arts. That is, if you feel that you do indeed have the case buttoned up."

"Tighter than a Christmas goose," he replied. "The answer is fairly clear in my mind."

"Capital. Would you be so gracious as to share it with me?"

"All in due time, old boy."

"What? That hardly seems fair," I protested. "After having been with you on this one from the beginning."

"But I don't want to spoil the surprise for you, Watson." He jabbed his knife into the plate of butter and smeared it on his biscuit. After taking a cautious bite, he masticated thoroughly before giving his head a minute shake accompanied with a smile of satisfaction. "I am going to have to convey my compliments to Mrs. Hudson. Her culinary abilities are beyond comparison. You really should endeavor to treat her with more politeness and regard, old boy. Lest she raise our rent."

He popped the rest of the biscuit into his mouth and continued chewing, a mocking smile evident on his lips.

"Quite right," I answered.

When he'd finished downing the morsel, he raised his index finger to emphasize his next point.

"In the morning we shall put my hypothesis to the test. And there is still the matter of how to best present it all tomorrow. But I have sent a message regarding that. Come, let's eat. And afterward, our glorious evening awaits."

We finished in plenty of time to change into our formal wear and catch a hansom to the Hall. Holmes anxiously tapped his fingers on the handle of his cane as we waited our turn to disembark from our cab in front of the magnificent structure. Once inside the atmosphere and setting were almost magical. The four balconies that rose up from the stalls, the spacious ground floor seating area which encircled the raised oval stage in the center of the hall, was truly breathtaking. The orchestra was set up on a platform on that stage to be seen and heard by all. The soft glow of the electric lights gave the extraordinary palace a heavenly appearance.

Our seats were a box on the Grand Tier above the first floor Loggia. As we settled into the plush red velvet chairs, I could see Holmes' eyes already drift away to a calmer place where he could escape from the constant workings of his remarkable mind. It was a pleasure to be seated beside him.

The concert was a magnificent diversion from disguises and confrontations, a gentlemen's night out that I positively enjoyed. We returned about eleven-thirty that evening. I bid Holmes a good night, knowing that Tuesday and the promised revelation to the mystery would no doubt prove to be a day that would be most memorable.

CHAPTER 16
THE BANQUETING HOUSE

I was up early Tuesday morning and entered the sitting room just as Mrs. Hudson was bringing in our breakfast. After exchanging pleasantries with her, I sat down at the table, barely able to see my plate and saucer underneath the dozen sheets of paper lying about its top.

"Am I having paper with my sausages, Holmes?"

"No, but you may eat with the satisfaction in the knowledge that I believe I've cracked the code of the second clue." His smile seemed to be stretched from ear to ear.

"Congratulations. What was the key in all that Latin on the side of the mausoleum?"

"It was most obviously the phrase that keeps getting repeated, 'In this sign thou shall conquer.' The cross, Watson. The sign of the cross."

I gingerly removed several of the sheets of paper from my place at the table and placed them on the side chair next to me.

"So, we are still looking for crosses? It shouldn't be too hard to find one in all of London," I said rather skeptically.

"Ah, but not one like this. It is the grandest of all crosses. Why, its name is a dead give-away. I'll give you time to finish your breakfast while I dress more appropriately for our trip."

He stood up and walked to the corner of the room to his table where he kept his make-up, wigs and prosthetics.

"Holmes, I haven't even begun to eat. Why don't we eat something together and you can tell me about your breakthrough?"

"I've no time to eat, Watson. My efforts spent the last few days were not in vain. It all begins with the translation of the Latin inscription from the mausoleum. Even though it was faded and not in classical Latin, I was able to make some sense of it. The first line is *In medio regnum.*' That roughly comes out to 'In the middle of the Kingdom.' So we must ask ourselves, what Kingdom?"

"What Kingdom indeed?"

I saw his reflection in his hand mirror smile. "Let us make the kingdom … Great Britain."

"All right." I consumed a bit of toast. Mrs. Hudson had browned it to the height of perfection. "Go on. I'm listening."

"And what should lie in the middle of Great Britain?" he said. "One must ask, is that meant to be geographical? Or social-political, perhaps?"

He paused, glanced at me, and raised an eyebrow.

"Why, it's the magnificent city of London, of course, that's the middle or center of Great Britain. And where is the center of London?" Again he paused, as if giving me time to consider the question, but before I could fashion a response, he continued. "In theory, it's Charing Cross. That is what is popularly agreed upon." He clapped his hands together as a smile crossed his lips.

"Charing Cross, Watson," he said. "None other than the spot where King Edward the First built the most expensive and largest cross monument in London, in memory of his wife, Eleanor of Castile." He stopped and let the words sink in. "The Eleanor Cross, an ornate stone monument built by the most prominent master Mason of the age. It stood in the center of London until Cromwell took it down. It was later replaced by the equestrian statue of Charles the First. Let us not forget that the last line of the Secret Anthology's Latin verse has always been 'In this sign thou shall conquer.' The sign of the cross."

"So that is the center of the Kingdom?"

"Yes, it has to be. And that's where we're going as soon as I'm finished here." He began applying powder to his cheeks and rouge to his lips.

"By the way, there's a letter by my seat. Can you make sure that we have Mrs. Hudson post it right as we leave? I do need an answer to it right away. It is a most urgent message that might provide me with the final bit information that I need to solve this case."

He put a long, gray wig upon his head and pulled it down on its side to straighten it. Then he placed his jacket and folded his deerstalker hat and placed them both into a valise. Quickly, he moved over to his wardrobe and threw a dress on his bed.

"That one's a bit too modern," he said, sorting through several other garments. Finally, he selected one and held it up for my viewing. "Ah, this is perfect. Does it look dowdy enough?"

The gingham dress that he had in front of him was indeed dowdy looking. Holmes turned towards me to model his choice.

"You look absolutely stunning, Holmes," I said. "That is, if you are going to help Mrs. Hudson scrub the floors today. What on earth are you doing?"

"I need a subterfuge to confuse our spies out there. Don't look out the window, but there are three groups of men gathered on opposite corners and one solitary man camped in the marketplace doorway keeping a close watch on our rooms. They wear their hats pulled low on their heads and one keeps a hood covering his face. Why, they might as well be wearing advertising boards if they wanted to be any more conspicuous. Any movement of ours will be closely monitored. I prefer to make our sojourn today alone without their company."

He slipped into the dress and stuffed some clothes into the bosom making it appear as if he had a pair of enormous breasts.

"A bit too buxom?" he asked.

"Why, certainly not," I retorted with a laugh.

Holmes then pulled a heavy black veil out of his armoire and draped it over his head.

"There," he said. "Do you think that this will hide my identity long enough to make them believe that Dr. Watson is escorting one of his elderly patients home?"

"Holmes, if I didn't know better, I'd think I was accompanying my dear old mother on a carriage ride."

"Splendid. I have my change of clothes in my bag. Don't forget my letter for Mrs. Hudson to post." He gestured toward his chair. "Now, are you ready Watson?"

"I certainly am," said I, taking a last bite of my toast and a quick sip of tea.

I went out first and flagged down a brougham. I was conscious that our surveyors were watching as behind me the now stooped, little old lady with a cane hobbled toward the curb. I helped the disguised Sherlock Holmes into the carriage so that his visage could be clearly seen through the cab window facing the street. Mrs. Hudson stood in the doorway and waved goodbye to us making the masquerade complete. With that we were off for the several miles ride to Charing Cross. Once safely out of sight, Holmes removed his disguise and changed back into his jacket and secured his hat firmly on his head.

"You would have gotten along quite well in the Elizabethan Age," I said, chortling. "Back in those days it was forbidden for women to get on the stage."

"A pity," he said, straightening his collar. "I much prefer leaving the distaff roles to the fairer sex." After glancing out of the window for several seconds, he smiled. "Good. It appears as though no one is following us. Now we have the day to ourselves."

The morning traffic was caught in the middle of its usual sluggish crawl, sending my friend into minor fits of agitation. He cursed the throngs of "wastrels and so called business men" cluttering up his streets. It took twice as long as usual to get to Charing Cross. Once there, Holmes sprung out of the cab leaving me to pay our driver and give him instructions to return the valise to 221 B Baker Street. I hurried to catch up to Holmes, his long, slender legs and walking stick moving in perfect unison as he strode purposefully through the crowd to the base of the bronze statue of Charles the First, seated upon his magnificent steed, both of which were perched atop an elaborately carved plinth.

"There, Watson," he said pointing his cane to the statue rising up above us. "Gaze upon the second answer to the translation of the Latin clue. The second line was 'A rege et sine coronum,' meaning 'a king without a crown'. Notice, if you will that King Charles does not have a helmet on. Quite unusual for a statue of a ruler riding into battle. He should, at least, be wearing a diadem or a crown on his head as befitting his rank. Yet there you have it. In the middle of the Kingdom, a King without a crown."

"Remarkable, Holmes. Truly remarkable. In all the times I've gazed upon this statue, I've never before noticed that the figure didn't have a helmet or a crown." I was suddenly as giddy as a lad searching for hidden eggs on Easter morning. "Where do we go from here?"

"There is still more to the inscription from the graveyard. We get the final direction from our mounted monarch. The last few lines were corrupted by the elements and the years. They were very tricky and convoluted. I went through many permutations before I settled on one with which I felt most comfortable. 'There he shall lead or point out.' It makes sense if you notice his right hand. He's holding a baton close to his saddle. It points straight ahead. His left hand is firmly clutching the reigns of his horse and is useless. The statue and his baton points south, down Whitehall towards the Banqueting House."

"Why the Banqueting House, Holmes?" I knew the history the place. It was also called the Palace of Whitehall, and had been constructed for elaborate entertaining. It was noted for the massive ceiling paintings by the classical painter, Peter Paul Rubens.

"It was the most difficult and time consuming of the verses to decode," Holmes said. "I was finally able to deduce its importance by the date of the Banqueting House's construction, which was 1622. After one of the many fires that the Whitehall Palace suffered, this classical reconstruction of the pavilion was completed on that date, and happens to coincide with another important date in the Templar tradition of the Iron Crown."

"And why is that date important?" I asked.

"Because one of the tales tracing the Iron Crown's journey with the Templars to England has it sailing to Britain in 1622. This particular trip records its journey quite clearly. If that is so, one could rightly say that its journey could have ended right here." He paused to stamp his foot. "If it is a coincidence, it's one that is too big to ignore. If you were to place the Crown someplace safe, why not inside a palace built for a king by the guild of Masons. The last line in the inscription is '*Maximum signum in occulis Dei*,' which I made out to be 'to the greatest sign under God's eye.' I suggest that King Charles the First here is directing us towards the Banqueting House. It's there we shall search for the greatest sign under God's eye, and our next clue. Come, Watson, the game is afoot."

After a brisk ten minute walk down Whitehall, we came upon the

Banqueting House. It was indeed a truly magnificent structure built by the Masons, who based the design on the Venetian concept of architecture with perfect symmetry. Their accomplishment was a classical building worthy of the Ancient Greeks or Romans, which had been a perfect setting for the royal court balls and reveries in times past. Its two-story structure, with seven sets of tall square windows, caught the glint of the morning sun. I was truly amazed to find that above the lintels of each window were alternating gables of either arches or triangles, indented with relief sculptures representing the Eye of Providence, the All-Seeing Eye of the Masons. Each was set in its own triangle, symbolizing God watching over us within the Holy Trinity. That was above all of the windows except the one in the center where there was the Templar Cross.

We stopped across the street from the building, oblivious to the throng of the people passing by. Holmes stood there transfixed, staring up at the side of the structure like a hawk eyeing his prey.

"Alas, we come to the final words in the Latin phrase," he said. "*In hoc signo vinces*—in this sign thou shall conquer."

We studied the edifice closely.

"Look at it, Watson. There it is." His voice was laden with subdued excitement. "To the greatest sign under God's eye. In this thou shall conquer ... God's All-Seeing Eye, carved in stone for all eternity."

I stared up at the intricately carved orb.

"And what is it watching?" he asked rhetorically. "The only symbol that is different ... The greatest sign of their religion ... The Templars' Cross, right there in the middle."

"My word," I gasped.

"Watson, I give you the Iron Crown." He pointed with his cane up at the center window's triangular gable.

"Great Scott, Holmes, do you mean that the Crown is buried above that window?" I could barely contain my astonishment.

"Yes, Watson, the Templars did their duty," he said. "If indeed it is the actual crown, the Masons did what they do best: preserve the relics of the past."

He shouldered his cane like a Royal Guardsman standing watch at the gate of Buckingham Palace. A smile of satisfaction lighted his face as the sun shone brightly on the Banqueting House. The throngs of people continued to pass by, unaware that the great Sherlock Holmes had solved one of the almost unfathomable of riddles.

"Now, no rest for the weary," he said, dropping his walking stick to his side." We must move on to the question of the three murders which confront us. Let's stop for a bite of lunch as I'm simply famished."

"I don't doubt that, the way you've been skipping meals lately."

"Good old Watson," he said. "Always my faithful friend, endeavoring to look after my welfare, despite my wayward ways."

"That's putting it mildly," I retorted.

His grin was expansive.

"After we eat," he said, "we shall return to Baker Street. I can't imagine the look of confusion on the faces of our group of watchers when they see the two of us return. They'll no doubt be quite bewildered and perplexed."

"Serves them right," I added.

We got a carriage and were off to lunch. We found a relatively new pub off of Church Street that we had seen advertised in the *Daily Telegraph*. Holmes ate a quick meal of fish and chips. Perhaps the treasure hunt had increased his appetite and the satisfaction of decoding the Secret Anthology had helped. I was most gratified to see him consuming some much needed nourishment. I made a mental note to attempt to persuade him to abide by a proper diet once this case was concluded. To do so now, I knew, would be fruitless.

Finding the hiding place of the Iron Crown in England was quite an achievement. On the way back to our quarters, he didn't seem to be concerned about the heaviness of the early afternoon traffic, either. His spirits were still elevated, and I let him bask in the afterglow of his significant accomplishment.

But the matter of the three murders niggled at me. Did he know the identity of the killer? If so, who was it?

There was much still to be answered.

As he'd said at the onset of today's journey, the game was afoot.

CHAPTER 17
THE MURDERER REVEALED

It was now half past one as we got ready to leave our loft at Baker Street. I reflected that it had been exactly one week since that dreary Tuesday morning that Inspector Hopkins had come to us with his request for assistance with the Masonic Lodge fire and subsequent murder of Dr. Withermew. So too, had it been exactly one week since we'd become entangled in the world of the Free Masons, the Templars, the Illuminati, the Thieves' Guild, and the Secret Anthology. Now, several murders and one treasure hunt for a holy relic later, Holmes was about to unwind the tangled knot of intrigue that had tied all of this together.

As I grabbed the unread morning paper from the sofa, I glanced down at the occasional table that held the four messages that Holmes had received in response to his own query the day before. The top one simply read, *Most certainly. You can use it any time.*

Shortly, Holmes and I were engaged in reading the morning papers. Well, I should say that I was busy reading the paper. My companion had moved his chair closer to the window and was holding the sheaf loosely in front of him, his head bobbing up and down barely taking in a word on each page.

"Holmes, is there something the matter?"

"Yes, there is. Edge over here and look outside at the street below."

I got up and moved over to the bay window.

"No, wait," he chided me. "Not with such obvious deliberation."

"What on earth are you talking about?" I said, taking my seat again.

He looked askance around the edge of his paper, and then made a tsking sound.

"There are only two groups of sentries out there on the street watching our quarters," he replied. "There should be four. This won't be complete unless all four are present. What is coming of this world when you can't depend on London's villains to be punctual anymore?"

He moved the curtain back slightly to get a better view of the street below.

"Ah," he said with a smile. "There he is. The last of our players. And just in time, no less."

I started to get up, but he waved for me to remain seated.

"Not now, Watson. The rest of our troop will be arriving at quarter to two as instructed, and they had better not be late. Timing is essential today, old boy." He folded his newspaper in front of him and pretended to read an article before he abruptly dropped it to the floor.

"I suggest we get our coats. It looks a bit nippy out there, judging from what the people below are wearing."

"Could catch a bit of the croup, if we're not careful," I said.

"Yes, very. And, Watson, would you mind bringing your Webley? It may come in handy."

We rose and after I retrieved my service revolver, put on our coats, our hats, our walking sticks, and proceeded to the door. Before exiting, however, Holmes darted off to the left and procured an ancient looking wooden chest, about the size of a hat box, from his laboratory table.

"Don't tell me you packed a lunch," I said.

"Hardly, Watson." He rapped his knuckles against the solid wooden frame. "This is our bait to trap The Hawk."

At the bottom landing we met Mrs. Hudson turning the corner ready to ascend the steps to retrieve the lunch tray.

"Ah, good afternoon to you, Mrs. Hudson," Holmes said cheerily. "As always, you're presence lends a bit of radiance to an otherwise dreary day."

The old girl's face puckered up with delight.

"Why thank you, Mr. Holmes," she said. "I must say, you're in a very good mood today."

Holmes moved past her and opened the door.

I sidled closer and whispered, "He's in an extraordinary good mood today. Let's hope nothing happens to spoil it."

We put our gloves on and stood on the curb taking in the brisk air. The news hawker on the corner waved his papers over his head and called out the headline in a bellicose tone, "Killers of Lawyers Captured. Read all about it."

"It's a shame, Holmes," I said, "that your name wasn't mentioned in the article in the apprehension of those killers."

"No, Watson, I'm perfectly happy to allow all the credit to go to Scotland Yard. We don't need any more enemies at the moment."

"Quite right. Makes perfect sense. Shall I get us a coach?"

"Not yet." He shifted the box to his other arm. "I'd rather we wait and make a production of greeting our guests on today's expedition."

Within a few minutes, a coach came down Baker Street and pulled up to our domicile.

Holmes smiled. "I see they all received my messages and are following my instructions to the letter. It's outstanding when one's plan comes together. Let us hope that the rest of it unfolds with similar precision."

Out stepped Inspectors Lestrade, Hopkins and Gregson, looking none too pleased about having had to share a cramped cab ride from Scotland Yard to Baker Street.

"This had better be worth the all this inconvenience, Holmes," Lestrade squawked. "Having to ride with these two blokes—"

"May I remind you that we're being watched, Lestrade? Pretend that you are glad to see me." Holmes grinned.

"Good morning, Mr. Holmes," said Hopkins as he stepped down from the brougham.

"Holmes." Gregson stepped down as well, tipping his bowler. "And I appreciate you rounding up those culprits the other night."

"Quite all right, old boy," Holmes said. "And now, good day, gentlemen. It is so nice to see you invigorated and so champing at the bit this fine afternoon. I trust you are ready to put this case to rest." He shifted the box to under his left arm and began heartily shaking each man's hand and even clapped Lestrade on the back.

"Hail, fellows, well met," he uttered loudly.

Then under his voice he whispered, "You did bring the extra sets of shackles as I had requested?"

"Yes," Hopkins replied while the other two merely nodded.

Holmes slapped Lestrade on the shoulder again for good measure. I was positive that this ostentatious show was for the benefit of our trio of spies.

"Let Dr. Watson and I secure a coach and we will be off to the location on London's north side that I sent you in the messages yesterday. You shall leave first. We will give you a good head start, and delay our arrival as much as possible. When you arrive there, please follow the instructions I gave you to the letter and secret yourselves around the foyer, completely out of sight. Wait for Dr. Watson and me to arrive. And make sure that your carriage is well hidden."

"All this had better come with a cherry on top of it," Lestrade muttered as he was feigning a wide smile.

"I assure you," Holmes said, with a smile mirroring that of the inspector, "that we shall sort out this affair to everyone's complete satisfaction."

Holmes and I went through another ritual of handshakes and grasping of arms as we sent them off.

After they had left, I signaled for a four-wheeler to pick up my companion and me. I got into the cab first and Holmes made a show of giving me the wooden box. I was surprised by the weight of it. Obviously, it contained something of substance. Holmes hopped into the cab and gave the driver the address and we pulled away. The box sat on the seat between us.

"Are you going to tell me what's inside of that?" I asked.

He smiled. "Of course. In due time."

Holmes glanced out of the window and watched the two sets of watchers and the solitary spy scramble for their own cabs.

"Driver," he called out, "do go extra slow on our trip. I don't want to lose any of our companions behind us."

"Got it, sir," the driver said.

I felt the pace of the coach slowing down.

"It is quite a procession we have, Watson."

"A veritable fool's parade," I said.

The afternoon traffic was turning into the customary mid-day congestion and Holmes' admonition to go slow was not really needed. We slowly wound our way through the streets of London headed north up Park Road to St. John's Wood. Holmes was leaning forward on his cane and humming one of the violin concertos from last night. As it was, he had plenty of time for a repeat performance.

"Now can you tell me what is going to happen next?" I finally asked.

"And spoil the surprise?" He arched an eyebrow. "You'll just have to have a little more patience, Watson. Trust me. We'll be there shortly."

"And where might that be," I asked.

"It's just up ahead. Do you remember the estate of Edward Oggelsby?"

The name had familiar ring to it.

"Yes," I answered. "He was the international banker whom you saved from ruin about a year or so ago, wasn't he?"

"You are correct."

I smiled at my accurate recollection. "It made for an interesting story in *The Strand*. I called it *The Case of the Hollow House*, as I recall."

"Yes, you wrote it up with your usual flare for hyperbole."

"So what does Oggelsby have to do with the resolution of this case?" I asked.

"Nothing," Holmes replied. "I asked him if he might be so kind as to let me borrow the use of his mansion today while he was at his place of business."

"His mansion? Whatever for?"

"I thought it would make an interesting setting in which to wrap up this case."

"Holmes, your grasp of the dramatic never fails to amaze me," said I. "Can't you do anything without making a big production out of it? I believe you must be the reincarnation of the stage director of the Globe Theater."

"'All the world's a stage,'" he said. "'And the men and women merely players.'"

He smiled at me and began to hum a different tune as we wound our way along the crowded streets. Periodically, he turned to check the progress of the four coaches behind us.

Many minutes later we turned into the tree-lined, cobblestone drive of a stately Georgian mansion of Edward Oggelsby. It was worthy of the setting of a penny dreadful novel. The landscaping was immaculate, just as I recalled it. Our carriage pulled through an elaborately fashioned metal gateway and then under a heavily vine-shrouded portico. We were met by an efficient looking man servant in an immaculate black uniform. Holmes got out slowly as if to make a production of it. I almost thought that I should bow to him when I exited the brougham

The man servant extended his open arms toward the box, but Holmes recoiled with an abruptness and shook his head.

The servant nodded accordingly and we followed him into the sumptuous mansion.

Once inside the grand foyer, he stopped and called out, "Lestrade, Hopkins and Gregson, respond in sequence. Are you all in place?"

Three sets of muffled assents resounded as each man stepped out into plain sight.

Holmes turned to me and winked.

"Our cavalry is standing at the ready," he said. "Now we must await the arrival of the three sets of hooligans who have followed us here."

"Why don't we just go out and arrest them when they get here?" Lestrade yelled.

"You have little flair for the dramatic, inspector," Holmes said. "It's better if they come to us. And besides, we still must await the apprehension of the principal villain."

"And who is that?" I whispered.

"Why, The Hawk, of course."

Holmes held up an extended index finger, waggled it, and shook his head minutely.

I frowned, knowing that he was toying with me, as well as the three Scotland Yard inspectors.

Everyone went back to his separate hiding place in the mansion's entrance. Lestrade and Hopkins secreted themselves behind two large pillars leading into the main anteroom. Gregson was on the other side crouching behind an enormous statue of King Neptune riding a pair of arching dolphin.

"Where's our hiding place?" I asked.

Holmes held his hand out toward the statue opposite Neptune. It was

He smiled and began to hum a different tune...

a marble rendition of Athena, replete with her bow, quiver, and atop her trusty steed. There was a screen next to it.

"May the goddess of the hunt protect us," Holmes said.

"Let's hope her aim is true if mine isn't," I said, patting the pocket that contained my Webley.

I was certain each of them was as much in the dark about the forthcoming events as I was. And I can only imagine how the spies outside were faring, trying to be stealthy while they were all tailing the same carriage without revealing themselves to each other.

A fool's parade indeed, I thought, and settled back to let Holmes direct the penultimate act of this unlikely drama.

Slowly, two men came creeping into the foyer, keeping close to the outer wall to avoid being seen. I recognized one of them immediately. He was Paul Merriweather, the Mason Grandmaster. The man with him was familiar as well. He'd been one of the Masons from the fight at the stable the other night where the two men had been killed. This second man had a small cudgel in his hand, while Merriweather had a larger blackjack in his.

Hardly a respectable weapon, I told myself.

As they circled around a tall, round Egyptian vase on a short pedestal, they both jumped in surprise as Gregson stepped out from behind King Neptune. The inspector drew his pistol and pointed it at the intruders.

"Get your hands up and keep your mouths shut," he commanded, and put the darbys on them and then walked the two of them toward the foyer in the next room.

"Do be quick about it," Holmes admonished. "This is only the first wave."

I frowned at Merriweather as the pair marched past us.

"Disgraceful," I muttered. "A man of your means and position…"

"Don't be too hard on the old boy, dear fellow," Holmes said. "I'm sure he had nothing but the most honorable of intentions."

"Yes, I'm sure as well," I said infusing the most sarcastic lilt as I could into my words.

"One pair down," Holmes said to me as we crouched behind a tall screen with a lotus-covered fabric front. I had my gun drawn as we stood ready for the next group.

We didn't have to wait long.

Less than three minutes later, the second two intruders came creeping along through the front door, not nearly as stealthily as the first couple had. They were tip-toeing down the center of the hall, looking cautiously both ways. No one moved to confront them until they had almost cleared the foyer. It was then that Lestrade and Hopkins both rushed out from behind their pillars and growled loudly at the pair telling them they were under arrest.

"This is an outrage," one of them sputtered with a French accent.

I burst out a laugh as I realized this one was the supercilious Duke Jean Pierre Bouchard, the Grand Master of the Knights Templars. The Duke carried some ineffectual looking sheathed saber that looked more decorative than functional. Lestrade ripped it from the Frenchman's side. The other man had the appearance of a servant of some sort and complied with all of the inspector's commands.

"*Au revoir*," Holmes said. "Or perhaps I should say, *abiento*?"

Bouchard's lip twisted into a scowl.

"I will have your jobs for this," he said to the inspectors.

"Buy a ticket and stand in line," Lestrade said. "Now get moving."

They put the irons on them right there, much to the chagrin of Holmes.

"Do be quick about it, inspectors," he urged. "We're still expecting more visitors."

They hauled the duo off into the mansion's interior to set them down with the first two intruders.

After we settled into another waiting posture I asked Holmes whom we were expecting next.

"It's difficult to say, Watson, but I imagine the Illuminati will be making their presence known before too much longer."

And he was correct. Only a scant five minutes or so had elapsed before another pair entered through the front door. It was Misters Cording and Cunningham, Cunningham's arm still being in a sling. They, unlike the others, carried no visible weapons, but rather a leather valise which the inspectors found to be full of cash. Also, in Mr. Cunningham's cummerbund was a small pistol.

"Obviously," Holmes said, "he brought all of his negotiating tools."

"We'll not forget this, Holmes," Cunningham said.

"Nor will I," Holmes retorted. "Now, take them away, gentlemen. We're still awaiting another set of guests."

"We've got one more?" I asked.

"Most assuredly," Holmes said as we watched Cunningham and Cording being taken to the next room to join the others. "When I was watching the procession trailing us from Baker Street, I saw four separate trackers. I have no doubt we still have one more major player en route."

"But who?" I asked.

"As I said, we've saved the best for last." He smiled. "It's The Hawk."

"But who the Devil is he?" I asked again, feeling frustrated.

"Wait," he said. "And you shall see."

With that, he said nothing more and took out his pipe.

A stage director to the last, I thought, and resigned myself to allow the ending to unfold.

However, several minutes went by and no one appeared.

"Holmes," I said. "Do you think that perhaps The Hawk isn't coming?"

Holmes arched his eyebrow once more and held a burning match over the bowl of his pipe. Waiting several moments, Holmes blew out a cloud of smoke and then spoke in a hushed tone.

"I believe. My dear Watson, that our wait is finally over, and all the players have gathered for the climax of this drama."

He pointed and I followed his gesture. Then, through the expansive glass windows on either side of the mansion's front door, I saw the hansom cab approaching. The driver pulled up to the front entrance and stopped. The door on the far side opened and three men got out. A fourth man ran up from the side and joined them.

"I saw one of those buggers jump from a cab perhaps fifty yards to our rear as we approached the gate in our brougham," Holmes said. "He obviously went to summon his confederates while the fourth man stood watch."

Their movements were obscured by the coach and their voices were muffled, but I could tell that one man, a rather large, athletic looking fellow, was giving the directions. When the coach departed there was no trace of the quartet.

"Get ready, Watson," Holmes said. "The final act is upon us. Stay here and be ready. I'll draw them out."

With that, he left our refuge behind Athena and began marching toward the front door, still carrying the wooden box.

"I'll take that, Mr. Holmes," a voice said. It had a strange familiarity to it, but I couldn't quite place it.

Great Scott, I thought. They'd already gained access to the house.

Holmes stopped with an exaggerated stupefaction.

"Are you addressing me?" he said in a loud voice.

"You know I am."

The large man stepped from behind one of the pillars.

It was then I received the shock of my life.

"So good of you to grace us, finally, with your presence, Dr. Hester," Holmes said. "Or do you prefer to be addressed as The Hawk?"

Hester stepped forward. He wore a dark suit and had a merchant's seaman's cap pulled over his hair. Three tough looking thugs flanked him. Two of them carried truncheons and the third was holding a large revolver that he had pointed at Holmes.

"I'll take that box," Hester said. "Now."

"This?" Holmes said, obviously putting a bit of relish in his tone. "Why, whatever for?"

"You know what for," Hester said. "That's the Crown, isn't it? You sent a message to the Pastor advising him that you'd deciphered the Anthology riddle." His voice had become almost maniacal with excitement. "Now give it to me."

Holmes posted a querulous expression, and then shook his head.

"I think not," he said. "Perhaps I shall merely set it on the ground and let you retrieve it."

Hester snorted in rage and told one of his companions to "Go fetch it."

As the man started forward Holmes bent over, as if to set the heavy box on the ground. Suddenly, his body sprang upward, and he hurled the box directly at the ruffian with the gun. The revolver discharged as Holmes did a pirouette, twisted, and fell.

Enraged, I stepped from around the statue, leveled my revolver, and fired.

The tough with the pistol grunted and grabbed his chest. He toppled over moments later.

Hester, in the meantime, lurched forward, grabbed the wooden box, and dashed off like a man possessed in the direction of the main gateway.

The two other ruffians began running also.

I yelled for them to halt and fired a round into the air. The two lackeys halted immediately, but Hester continued his flat-out sprint.

"I'll get him, Watson," Holmes said, jumping to his feet.

I prayed that he hadn't been struck by the thug's bullet. I was suddenly joined by Gregson and Lestrade.

"What in blazes is all the shooting?" Lestrade asked.

"Never mind that," Gregson said, and yelled for the two thieves to prostrate themselves on the ground. They both complied.

As the two inspectors ratcheted on the manacles, I gazed outward, watching the ungainly foot race between Holmes and his foe. Hester, while appearing more athletic, had the burden of carrying the heavy wooden box. Holmes, on the other hand, was not burdened by such and had an overall slimmer frame, which afforded him more speed. Hester was nearing the ornate gateway when the detective overtook him.

The tackle was worthy of a championship rugby match. Holmes drew abreast of his opponent, reached out, and thrust his body in front of the other man's. The two of them tumbled forward, pell-mell, rolled with double summersaults on the lush grass. Both attempted to scramble to their feet. I ran toward them as quickly as my war wounds would allow, and observed the ensuing hand-to-hand encounter unfold like the flickering display of pictures in a nickelodeon.

Hester lurched forward swinging his right fist like a mace. Holmes parried the blow with his left arm and sent a quick right-handed punch to the other man's face. Hester's head jerked back and Holmes then stepped forward and delivered another punch to the bigger man's side. Stiffening in obvious pain, Hester lashed out, catching Holmes with a back-handed blow that sent the detective staggering backward three steps.

I struggled to quicken my pace, but my obsolescent legs would go no faster.

Recovering first, Hester bent down and reached for the wooden box. Holmes sprang forward and smashed his left knee into Hester's side. I was almost close enough now to hear the expulsion of the villain's breath. Rearing upward, Hester cocked his arm back to deliver a blow, but this time Holmes was ready. He stepped inside the other man's extended arms and delivered two twisting punches to the abdomen. Hester's body curled forward, and Holmes brought an uppercut to the other man's face, and then grabbed him and flipped him forward with some sort of jiu-jitsu movement.

Hester literally flew over Holmes body and landed on his back with a resounding thud. He made no movements after that.

By this time I was next to my friend, who was smiling with satisfaction.

"My God, Holmes," I said. "Are you all right?"

"Quite so, Watson," he said. "A bit of physical activity after lunch is always most invigorating."

"But," I said, surveying his chest. "That bugger shot you. I saw him."

Holmes raised an eyebrow and began patting his chest and stomach.

I saw no traces of blood, but then spotting a hole in the left side of his jacket where the thug's bullet had passed through.

"Close, as the circus people say," Holmes retorted. "But no cigar."

"Just let me be the judge of that," I said, feeling his side to be certain there was no actual wound.

"All in good time, old boy," he said, brushing my hand away. "First things first."

With that, he glanced down at his vanquished foe and then stepped over to the wooden box. It had a hinged top and latch, which was secured by a tiny lock. Holmes made a show of patting his pockets before smiling and coming up with a small key. He stooped down and slid the key into the lock. As he was opening the box Hester started to come around. His eyes glanced to Holmes, and then to me, and then to the box.

"I wouldn't advise you trying to make scratch and start round two," my companion said. "My dear friend, Dr. Watson here is an exceptional marksman."

Hester looked back to me, and then his gaze returned to the box.

"At least let me see it," he said.

"Most certainly," Holmes said, lifting the lid. "In fact, I'll be glad to let you wear it."

Hester's eyes widened, and then his face fell as Holmes pulled out a pair of heavy, iron manacles from the box. He glanced at me with an expression of glee, and then grabbed Hester's right wrist and slipped the first restraint in place.

"But the crown," Hester said. "You sent that message to Thaddeus saying you'd found it."

"A mere ruse," Holmes said. "An iron ruse, to catch a crafty bird of prey. A hawk."

"This one's the Hawk?" Gregson asked, coming abreast of us.

"Yes," Holmes said. "The leader of the Thieves' Guild, called so due to his aquiline nose, no doubt."

Gregson frowned and grabbed the now restrained Hester.

"Come along, you bugger," he said. "We got a good place for you at the Yard."

Hester ignored him. "Holmes, did you actually decipher the code?"

The detective said nothing.

"Please," Hester continued. "I've got to know."

"Some things," Holmes said, looking at me, "Are best left mysteries for the ages, eh, Watson?"

Gregson shoved Hester toward the house. I leaned close to Holmes.

"That was a bit of a surprise," I said. "I would have never suspected him."

"Oh, come now, Watson," Holmes said. "It was painfully obvious."

"It was? When did you suspect him?"

"When we were attacked by that group of ruffians in North Wickham," he said. "They mentioned The Hawk, remember?"

"Of course," I said. "But they didn't mention his name."

Holmes chuckled. "Nor did they have to do so. Hester was the only person, aside from the inspectors, who initially knew we were working on deciphering the Anthology. You'll recall his visit to us in which he professed his dubious concern for poor old Pastor Thaddeus... Thus, he was the only one who knew to have his lackeys follow us to monitor our progress."

"But I still don't see the association," I said. "How did you know Hester was The Hawk?"

Holmes smirked and raised his index finger to his own nostril.

"Many times, you may remember," he said. "I have made the pronouncement that prominent men have prominent noses."

"Do you mean?"

"Yes," he said, grinning broadly. "His rather distinctive proboscis, aquiline in shape, is the veritable incarnation of a raptor's beck."

I burst out a laugh.

Hester muttered a curse.

"Amazing," I said. "Simply amazing." I continued to marvel at his peerless deductive abilities as we watched Gregson push Hester toward the front entrance of the mansion. I felt ebullient that we'd captured all of the evil doers, but at the same time I was a trifle bit dismayed that I had missed the obvious clue. But then again, everything seemed obvious after one of the detective's explanations.

We escorted Hester back across the lawn, with Holmes carrying the now-empty wooden box like a trophy. While we waited for the Bobbies and the wagon, the inspectors assembled all of the prisoners on the front steps of the mansion. Seated at the end were the two Masons, one looking defiant while the second stared dejectedly downward. Next to them were Broussard and his assistant sitting side by side on the next level of steps, and finally Cording and Cunningham, who were seated on the bottom level. Hester took his place on the other end sitting on the top step.

"So these are all of the ones who followed you here today?" Gregson asked.

"More or less," Holmes said. "Each group had employed a watcher to survey the movements of Watson and myself. When they spied me carrying the wooden box and heading here ..." He paused and held it up. "They immediately went back and told their confederates where we were. Thinking that I had, indeed, solved the riddle and obtained the crown, by virtue of a series of messages I'd arranged to be delivered, they all swarmed to this location in hopes of obtaining the treasure."

Holmes smiled slyly, opened the lid of the box, and held it upside down.

"Let this serve as a good reminder to all of you gentlemen that one should always assess a pronouncement with the proper amount of skepticism."

"In other words," I couldn't resist adding, "It's foolish to count your chickens before they're hatched."

Holmes arched and eyebrow and shot me a withering glance.

"My dear fellow," he said. "I hope that clichéd remark isn't indicative of your next literary rendition."

"And what was the reason for that big send off back at Baker Street, Mr. Holmes?" said Hopkins, moving to the end of the steps to stand next to the Masons.

Lestrade simply had a grin on his face, no doubt satisfied that he stood over a catch of suspects. I was certain he was not exactly sure what all they were suspected of, but none the less, he relied on the fact that they were all suspects brought together by the genius of Sherlock Holmes.

The detective marched triumphantly in front of the captive group.

"Inspectors," Holmes said. "You have before you an interesting quartet. A duo of not-so-free Masons, a set of unmatched Templars, two very non-illuminated Illuminati, and a criminal known as The Hawk, who was manipulating several supposed secret organizations as easily as moving chess pieces on a checkered board."

The captives all seemed to glare at Hester simultaneously.

Holmes laughed at this unified action.

"Come, come, gentlemen," he said. "Don't be too harsh on the poor fellow. His wings have been clipped."

"Who is he?" Lestrade asked.

"May I present," Holmes said, extending his hand, "Dr. Samuel Hester, the attending physician and supposed confidant of one, Pastor Ezra Thaddeus. The Pastor, a Mason, is a very sick man who is well versed in the lore of the Secret Anthology and the Iron Crown."

"That blasted magic crown again?" Gregson said.

"Quite," retorted Holmes. "It is the Iron Crown that brings all of these men together here today."

"But how does it all tie together, Mr. Holmes?" Hopkins queried.

Holmes moved so that he was standing centered in front of the captives.

"It is also the motive for at least three murders," he pronounced loudly pointing his walking stick down the row at every one of the seated criminals.

I put my revolver back into my jacket pocket and stepped off to the side to observe, knowing that Holmes was about to begin what I knew was going to be the brilliant summation of the past week's work.

"To answer your question first, Inspector Hopkins, since we began with the fire at the Masonic Temple and the murder of Dr. Withermew, the prize spoken of in the Secret Anthology has long been the end game prize for the Masons, the Templars, the Illuminati, and, of late, the Thieves' Guild, run by Dr. Hester." He paused and arched an eyebrow. "Otherwise known as The Hawk."

All eyes turned toward him and Hester's face twisted into a fierce scowl.

"What are you all looking at?" he spat.

"Those were the four parties most interested in the Iron Crown," Holmes said. "Once Dr. Watson and I became involved, we became the center of their attention, as they hoped that we would be successful in unlocking the complex Latin cipher within the Secret Anthology. So, it was natural that our every move was to be shadowed as they all rightly assumed that, in addition to solving the murders that were piling up, we would also turn our attention to finding the Iron Crown."

"The Iron Crown," Lestrade said. "Is that what all these murders have been about?"

"Correct," Holmes said. "And then some."

"But why?" Lestrade persisted. "What is the blasted thing, anyway?"

"All in good time, Inspector," Holmes replied. He turned back to address the group, a headmaster addressing his students. "And now, to address your very cogent query, Hopkins, the charade of the over exuberant send off at Baker Street was to give the impression that we were very delighted about something and wanted to congratulate Scotland Yard. We were then dismissing all of the inspectors involved in the cases who might possibly have anything to do with the murders *and* the Iron Crown. We wanted them to think that we were sending you on your merry way, and we were proceeding to collect the spoils of our victory." He paused and shot an intense stare at Hester. "Presumably the Iron Crown."

He tapped his cane against the wooden box.

Hester's face twisted with impotent rage. "Damn you, Holmes."

"And…" The detective smiled beatifically. "As you can see, it worked like a charm."

"So, what are we to do with this lot?" Lestrade asked scratching his head with his free hand.

"After I am done with my explanation, you will arrest the murderer of our three victims and charge the remainder of these despicable charlatans with conspiracy to commit a theft and the unlawful entry into this residence." He canted his head. "Unless, that is, you wish to release them all so that they may convey to the world that crime, indeed, does not pay, especially when confronted by Scotland Yard."

"Not much chance of that," Lestrade mumbled. "They don't deserve any free passes."

"Agreed," Gregson said. He turned to Hopkins, who gave an emphatic nod of his head.

Holmes began to pace in front of his captive audience. His eyes were sharp and his voice was as clear and finely honed as that of an eloquent orator. He stopped at the end of the group, looking down at the Mason, who had a defiant look still etched on his brow.

"Let's begin with the night at the Masonic Temple. I know that Mr. Tobias was not there to rob or murder Dr. Withermew, but rather to speak to him about the importance of *protecting* the Secret Anthology." He smiled. "You see, Mr. Tobias claimed that he was overly concerned that the Anthology wasn't being securely guarded by Withermew, and he was there to plead with him to take greater pains to safe guard it." He paused a flashed a wry smile. "Ostensibly, that is."

This surprised me. I had no idea that Tobias had had an alternative motive.

Both of the Mason's heads jutted upward toward Holmes.

"What do you mean?" one of them asked.

"Merely that your trusted fellow Mason, Randall Tobias, had less than altruistic motives."

"You're lying," the one Mason said. "Randall was a good bloke."

"He was one of us," the other one added.

"He was also an inveterate gambler," Holmes said. "With a yen for opium. The Pastor confirmed this. To support his habitual and addictive vices, Tobias needed a substantial amount of money. He'd already run afoul of barrister Langhorn and the Illuminati running up his debts. Who knows what other pressures came to bear. So he had a pressing need to procure the Secret Anthology so that he could properly copy the pages concerning the location of the Iron Crown. These, he knew, would be extremely valuable to the right people. He then intended to sell this information to the other interested parties, namely the Templars and the Illuminati."

The Mason swore. "May he rot in hell."

"I'm sure he's there anxiously awaiting your eventual arrival so he can beg your forgiveness." Holmes waited while the two Masons grumbled to themselves. "What needs to be established, in terms of laying out the diagram of the entire series of crimes, was who else knew about his presence at Withermew's office?"

Holmes paused again. He was obviously enjoying this recounting, knowing that he had the undivided attention of all of us.

"That question was answered by the little trip that I made the previous afternoon," he said. "Merely to confirm what I had already suspected."

Hester's frown thickened.

"Yesterday," Holmes said, "I went out, it was to St. Mary's Hospital to visit Pastor Thaddeus. As I had hoped, the good pastor was alone, as Dr. Hester usually only visited him in the morning. He was semi-lucid, so I asked him if anyone had been there on Monday and Tuesday mornings when Thaddeus heard Tobias's final confession." His gaze turned toward Hester. "He recalled that you were there."

"This is preposterous," Hester said.

Holmes spun and pointed his walking stick to the end of the row toward the infamous Doctor Hester.

"Don't try to deny it," Holmes said. "Upon overhearing on Monday that Tobias was going to visit Dr. Withermew to convince him of the necessity to let him make a copy of the Secret Anthology since the Pastor's memory was fading, you realized that this would be your only chance to steal it for yourself. You were familiar with Tobias's unsavory proclivities, namely his gambling and opium use, from your work in the East End Medical Clinic. Thus, you realized the potential financial windfall should you be able to obtain the Anthology, or one of the copies. It had to be you who was the hooded, second intruder that night at Withermew's office. It was you who struggled with him in the doorway to the library and knocked over the candelabra. It was you who repeatedly hit him in the head with a cudgel in your right hand, killing him." Holmes waved his cane at Hester in an accusatory fashion; a long pointed finger. "When you discovered that Tobias had preceded you, you fled."

"That's absurd," Hester said. "You'll never prove it."

"Won't I?" Holmes regarded the man with an expression of distain. "Tuesday morning, on your regular visit to Pastor Thaddeus, you overheard Tobias informing him that he'd given the Anthology to Chief Polk so that he could make a copy of the Latin riddle detailing the location of the Iron Crown. You then went to Polk's house to retrieve it, and ended up killing him when he wouldn't reveal its location to you."

Hester's lips drew into a tight line. He said nothing.

"Fearing discovery," Holmes said, "you left after conducting a hasty and inadequate search. Your objective then shifted to gaining control over the copy that Polk had made for Tobias. What you didn't know at the time was that Polk was both a Mason and a Templar. He not only made one copy of the Anthology's riddle for Tobias, erroneously believing that it was to be turned over to Pastor Thaddeus, but he sent one to Duke Jean Pierre Bouchard as well."

"That traitor," Bouchard mumbled.

"Shut your yap," Gregson shouted.

"This is ridiculous," Hester protested. "One can't believe the ramblings of Thaddeus. I told you, he's nothing but a senile old fool."

"One can when it is corroborated by the hospital attendant to whom I spoke yesterday when I visited Thaddeus. The attendant told me that you looked in on Thaddeus every morning at about half past seven. And he remembers Tobias being there on Tuesday at a quarter past eight the same time he brought breakfast in. Yes, and Thaddeus was quite adamant that you were always there whenever Tobias made his confessions or lurking about whenever he and Tobias spoke in private." Holmes paused and cast a wry smile. "Concerned about your elderly charge being taken advantage of by the unscrupulous Randall Tobias, were you?"

Holmes paused and took in a deep breath. Hester made no reply.

"Your dedication to the welfare of your patient is most admirable," Holmes said, his tone laden with sarcasm. "All part of your elaborate subterfuge. But who would suspect a loyal, selfless physician, the faithful caretaker of his elderly, demented charge? Any ill will or malicious intent would hardly be possible." Once again Holmes stressed the obvious irony. He slowly walked towards the accused, who began to struggle in his cuffs.

"Hold still, you aren't going anywhere," Gregson said placing his hand on Hester's shoulder.

"Thaddeus told me that he remembered that he asked you to stay and pray with him for Tobias's soul," Holmes said. "You complied with his wishes, which is why it wasn't until a little past eleven that you made it to Polk's house and confronted him, as verified by the broken clock. Once again, when direct questioning and threats didn't work, you resorted to violence and clubbed him. Then you took your time tearing his home apart searching for the Secret Anthology. You looked everywhere except where he had put it for temporary safe keeping."

Hester's eyes widened. "Where? Where was it?"

Holmes lifted his pant leg and tapped the end of his cane against the sole of his shoe.

"It was in his trusty boot."

"In his boot!" Hester yelled. "You're saying the idiot hid the damn Anthology in his boot?"

"Quite right," Holmes said. After a few beats of silence, he continued. "Your timing was a bit tardy the entire way. You went after the Anthology the same night that Tobias was there trying to convince Withermew to give it to him. Not only did you arrive after Tobias had just left, but you arrived at Polk's after he'd copied the Anthology and given one to Tobias, ostensibly for Thaddeus, and sent the other out by messenger."

"But how did you come to suspect me?" Hester asked.

"I suspected that something was amiss after your visit to Baker Street inquiring as to our progress on the Anthology."

The detective leaned close into Hester's face with his steely, unflinching glare. The villain's breathing was quick and shallow. "It's understandable why you had to kill both Dr. Withermew and Chief Polk, but what about Tobias?"

Hester frowned. He obviously knew the game was up. "The fool was weak. After the murders he going to go to the police and confess everything about the Secret Anthology." He licked his lips and coughed dryly. "After finding nothing at Polk's house, a couple of my legion from the Thieves' Guild tracked Tobias down at his home later that evening. When I arrived, he was a nervous wreck. I made sure that he consumed all of the brandy that he had in his house and I prodded him, trying to get him to reveal where the original Anthology was at Polk's. I didn't know that Scotland Yard had discovered Polk's body yet. I thought that I would have time to go back and take it from where ever Tobias and Polk had hidden it."

Hester licked his dry lips again. His head sagged down and his voice cracked as he continued. "But Tobias didn't know where Polk might have hidden it. He confessed that he'd sold a copy to the Illuminati to alleviate his gambling debts. He told me that Polk had also sent a copy to the Templars. I was furious that I'd let another copy get away from me. So, I stabbed him and rolled him up in his carpet, tying both ends together. We went out to the street and waited until I spotted a hay wagon making a late night delivery. I flagged down the driver and offered him twenty pounds if he would help us drop the carpet off somewhere. Fortunately, he was a man of little scruples and agreed to do it. I let him keep the carpet."

"And you dropped the body behind the building belonging to the Templars?"

Hester glanced at Duke Jean Pierre Bouchard and laughed. "It seemed fitting since he'd had a copy of the Anthology sent to him by Polk." He lifted his head and smiled.

"But Tobias was not quite dead. He managed to mutter a dying declaration as his body was subsequently found," Holmes said. "One that eventually led me to you."

Hester spat out a derisive exhalation.

"Three murders for an Anthology that so many people had knowledge of." Holmes stared into Hester's eyes with a fierce intensity like two burning coals. "It is easy to comprehend the reasoning of the Masons, the Templars and even the Illuminati... They all wanted the Secret Anthology for similar reasons." He arched an eyebrow and glared at Hester. "But why you? What was your reason?"

Hester's face twisted into an expression of sheer contempt and hatred. "Isn't it obvious, Mr. Holmes?"

"I do have my suspicions," Holmes answered. "But I think you owe all of us present an explanation. If you would be so inclined."

He seemed to consider the request for several seconds, and then snorted out a laugh.

"It's said the Iron Crown can absolve its possessor of all his sins. Those pathetic zealots really believe that nonsense. They would die for it. To be able to lay my hands on the most holy of relics... Do you know how much something like that would be worth to these religious fools?" Hester was almost panting for breath now. "Why, they'd pay a veritable fortune for it. I could have been rich."

"Not this time, I'm afraid." Holmes said. "Hopkins, Lestrade, Gregson... There is your murderer."

"So it was him," Hopkins said. "He was hoping to obtain the Iron Crown and then sell it to the highest bidder."

"The Illuminati, the Masons and the Templars," Lestrade said. "All three would've paid top dollar for it."

"Simply one man driving this whole thing," I said.

"And leaving three dead bodies in his wake," Holmes said.

Hester lowered his head.

"But all these clandestine groups," Lestrade said. "I still don't understand the reason for all of those secret societies."

"To make sense of the patterns of existence," Holmes began, "to fabricate connections trying to explain away the seemingly unexplainable directions that life takes, man seeks to create a believable chain of events.

He sees conspiracies and plots where there are none."

"And all the while we were thinking that this was all based on some religious fervor," I said. "When instead, it was just simple avarice."

"Which is still one of the seven deadly sins, Watson," Holmes retorted. "But, as usual, you're absolutely correct. The thread of greed was woven through this case, from beginning to end."

"I still don't see how you put it all together," Lestrade said.

Holmes, who had a broad smile on his face, raised his index finger in the manner of the headmaster delivering the final lecture of the day to his students.

"Inspector, an investigation is simply a succession of reason, facts, deduction and conclusions; all separate waiting for interpretation." He paused for emphasis. "So as I've often said in the past, eliminate the impossible, and whatever is left, no matter how improbable, must be the truth. No labyrinthine conspiracies, no secret societies. Simply the truth."

"But what about the Mason and Templar's Secret Anthology?" said Gregson.

"Ah, the map to the actual location of the Iron Crown," Holmes said. "That's quite another matter."

I watched as the eyes of all of the captives locked upon the detective. A smile jerked up the corner of his mouth as he took his time lighting his pipe. Finally, he shook out the match and straightened up, expelling a cloudy breath as he spoke.

"Are those flanges contained within it the nails from the True Cross upon which they crucified the Christ?" He wrinkled his brow in mystification. "Did it protect Emperor Constantine from harm, as the tale goes?" Again, he paused and appeared reflective. "And does it hold the mystical power to forgive all of a man's sins?"

Holmes smiled after this last statement. "That is a matter of faith, gentlemen."

"But where is it?" Hester cried out. "Where?"

"As far as the actual physical crown," Holmes answered. "Who knows? Perhaps it is in the cathedral outside of Milan ..." He cast a quick look my way. "Or could it really be hidden here in England? The true crown... No one really knows."

"Then you didn't really solve it?" Hester demanded.

Gregson gave the man's head a slap to shut him up.

Holmes blew out a plume of smoke. "The clues are vague, misleading, obtuse, and written in the poorest of Latin. If, indeed, England does harbor the real Iron Crown brought back by the Templars, then I'm afraid it is lost to time. We'll just have to assume that the actual crown is on display at the Cathedral of Monza outside of Milan. There it can be seen. There it shall stay."

A smile crept across his lips as he turned towards me and winked.

THE END.

THE STORY BEHIND THE STORY
BY RAY LOVATO

I've always been fascinated by secret societies; those clandestine cabals that control our fate from behind the scenes, those conspiracy theories that are woven through the fabric of our lives, secretly guiding our destinies from the shadows.

The Illuminati—that top one percent that rules our world today. The Knights Templar—the ancient Christian warriors who fought Crusades and plundered holy relics, bringing them back to England for safe keeping. Or the political reach of the Free Masons, and the legend of their being responsible for building our nation's capital and the layout of Washington, D.C. So I set out to write about one of these secret societies in my Sherlock Holmes' novel. But then I thought, why limit myself to just one of these societies when I could write about all three? So, I did.

Every writer of Holmes is intrigued by the relationship between Sherlock and the Chief Inspectors of Scotland Yard, that delicate balance-between friend and foil, each fulfilling their distinct function in the story. Lestrade, Gregson and Hopkins are all reasonably capable but never able to keep up with the Great Detective. It is always interesting to see how they interact with Holmes. But which one do I include in my Sherlock Holmes novel? Why not include them all? So, I did.

The Iron Crown of Lombardy, a holy relic and a priceless treasure, made the perfect item for everyone to pursue. And London was so generous and obliging with its landmarks Charing Cross, the statue of Charles the First, and the Banqueting House to complete the riddle of the Secret Anthology. Plus, I finally got to put my four years of Latin from high school to some use.

THE REAL STORY BEHIND THE STORY

Not everyone is fortunate enough to have a best friend to share their childhood with since they were six years old. I was blessed to have Mike Black and experience a lifetime of adventures. So when it became time for me to write my first Sherlock Holmes novel, it had to be a shared experience with Mike.

We have collaborated and co-plotted on several Doc Atlas stories before. We would write alternating chapters or fill in parts that we wanted inside of each other's chapters, adapting our styles to complement each other.

The Adventure of the Iron Crown was an entirely different experience. I basically wrote a novella. Well, it was really more of an extended outline with many words hung on it. Then Mike took over, adding brilliant passages of dialogue, extending scenes, fleshing out characters and turning the novella into a novel. The true credit belongs to him.

It was like playing together in the sand box in Mike's backyard those many years ago.

My best friend has always been there for me.

Ray Lovato

ADDENDUM

By Michael A. Black

As usual, Ray gives me way too much credit. When Ron Fortier first suggested that Ray and I take a stab at writing a Sherlock Holmes novel, the idea seemed pretty daunting. We'd both written short stories featuring the peerless Holmes and Watson, but maintaining the mystery and suspense for a novel-length project was another matter entirely. However, we were determined to give it a go. It began with Ray emailing me that he had an idea for a novel that might work. It involved the secret societies and a valuable hidden treasure. I told him it sounded promising, and he immediately went to work. In all of our long association together, I don't think I've ever seen him work as hard as he did on *The Adventure of the Iron Crown*. He sent me the story and said it needed a little fleshing out here and there. I sat down and started to read and was immediately pulled into it.

But let me backtrack a little.

As Ray mentioned, he and I grew up together on the South Side of Chicago. We lived across an alley from each other. We spent innumerable times going back and forth between each other's houses, playing in the neighborhood, and inevitably outwitting all of the other kids. It was like we were somehow psychically connected. There was an unspoken bond between us, and we knew how to read each other perfectly. Our nickname in the neighborhood was "The World's Finest," alluding to the Superman/Batman comic books.

Being able to work on this novel with him brought back the memories of those good old days. Ray gave me a manuscript that was so well written that all I had to do was add a few bits here and there. Despite his protestations to the contrary, the main credit should definitely go to him. (I took Spanish in high school instead of Latin, and I could have never figured out the complexities of those secret organizations like he did.)

The result, I hope, is a bit reminiscent of the Sherlock Holmes novels of the master, Sir Arthur Conan Doyle, who gave us the greatest consulting detective of all, and his stalwart associate, Dr. John H. Watson.

The Adventure of the Iron Crown is an homage to them, from another pair of stalwart partners, Raymond Louis James Lovato and Michael A. Black.

ILLUSTRATRATIVE

BY ROB DAVIS

From time to time in the history of Airship 27 Productions publications fans have been enlightened as to the processes used to create and assemble our books. To that end Airship Captain Ron Fortier encouraged me to write a short piece about how a couple of the interior illustrations in this book came about.

On page 83 of this book you'll find an illustration of Sherlock Holmes instructing his minions, which he calls his "Irregulars." As I was doing the research necessary to assure proper fashion, furniture and fixtures I happened across an illustration of Dr. Watson addressing the Irregulars from the novel *A Study In Scarlet*. (the signature appears to be "Rich Clineschmidt, though I imagine someone with more knowledge may correct me). With a few changes and embellishments I created the scene with Holmes giving marching orders to his motley troops.

On page 100 you'll find Captain Ron's admitted favorite illustration that includes the three Scotland Yard Inspectors in heated argument being scolded by Holmes while Watson observes. Once again I discovered an illustration that had just the right setting (unfortunately the signature is truncated and only "Arthur" can be completely deciphered, though I believe it is also from *A Study in Scarlet*, and most likely a different edition)

167

and once more I adapted and embellished to create the illustration.

The resultant pieces are admittedly "swipes" of existing work. Some people use the word "swipe" with derogatory disdain. I respectfully point readers to the fact that no less a luminary than Vincent Van Gogh "swiped" from prints and previous paintings in his work. I'm no Van Gogh but I hope I'm allowed the same artistic license he employed.

Thanks, as always, for your continued support of our efforts at Airship 27 Productions!

Rob Davis, December 11, 2021

About Our Creators

Writers

MICHAEL A. BLACK - is the award winning author of 47 books, most of which are in the mystery and thriller genres. He has also written in sci-fi, western, horror, and sports genres. A retired police officer, he has done everything from patrol to investigating homicides to conducting numerous SWAT operations. Black was awarded the Cook County Medal of Merit in 2010. He is also the author of over 100 short stories and articles, and wrote two novels with television star, Richard Belzer (*Law & Order SVU*). His Executioner novel, *Fatal Prescription*, won the Best Original Novel Scribe Award. His latest novels are the *Trackdown* series (*Devil's Dance, Devil's Fancy, Devil's Brigade,* and *Devil's Advocate*) and *Legends of the West* (under his own name), *Dying Art* and *Cold Fury* (under Don Pendleton), and the Gunslinger series (*Killer's Choice, Killer's Brand, Killer's Ghost, Killer's Gamble,* and *Killer's Requiem*) under the name A.W. Hart.

RAYMOND LOUIS JAMES LOVATO - loves writing pulp fiction with his lifelong friend, author Michael A. Black. Ray also enjoys traveling the world with his lovely wife, Susan. Years ago, on a five-hour flight to Saint Martin, he was inspired to draft an homage to Doc Savage, the Man of Bronze. After presenting the first chapter as a birthday gift to his best friend they continued to write projects together including *The Adventures of Doc Atlas*, a host of short stories, and this Sherlock Holmes novel, *The Adventures of the Iron Crown*.

Interior Illustrations

ROB DAVIS - began his professional art career doing illustrations for role-playing games in the late 1980s. Not long after he began lettering and inking, then penciling comics for a number of small black and white comics publishers. Most notably Rob worked for Eternity Comics (which eventually became Malibu Comics in the 1990s) on their book SCIMIDAR with writer R.A. Jones. Branching out to other black and white publishers and eventually working at both DC and Marvel. Rob worked on likeness intensive comics like TV adaptations of QUANTUM LEAP and STAR TREK's many incarnations mostly on the DEEP SPACE NINE comics for Malibu. At Marvel he worked on the Saturday morning cartoon adaptation PIRATES OF DARK WATER. After the comics industry implosion in the late 1990s Rob picked up work on video games, advertising illustration and T-shirt design as well as some small press comics like ROBYN OF SHERWOOD for Caliber.

Rob continues to do the occasional self-published comic book and as publisher and designer for his small-press production REDBUD STUDIO COMICS. As well look for Kickstarter fundraisers for his work with SILVERLINE COMICS on TWILIGHT GRIMM with writer R.A. Jones. Rob is Art Director, Designer and Illustrator for the New Pulp production outfit AIRSHIP 27 partnered with writer/editor Ron Fortier.

Rob is the two time recipient of the PULP FACTORY AWARD for "Best Interior Illustrations" since 2010 for his work on SHERLOCK HOLMES: CONSULTING DETECTIVE. He works and lives in central Missouri with his wife, two children and soon to be first granddaughter!

COVER ARTIST

MORGAN FITZSIMONS—is a British traditional artist and illustrator. Born in the North of England in 1939, she has been drawing and painting since she could hold a brush. Morgan studied at what is now the LJMU (Liverpool John Moores University). Her work can be found at: @morganfitzsimons.art ; http://www.morganfitzsimons.com ; and https://www.pinterest.com/nicpoh/morgan-fitzsimonscom/

THE OTHER WATSON

In 2009 Airship 27 Production launched its series of brand new Sherlock Holmes adventures titled "Sherlock Holmes – Consulting Detective." Among the contributors was a British writer named I.A. Watson. Considered a good omen by the publishers to have Watson on board, that first volume became a huge success; as did the subsequent sequels.

In the past 12 years I.A. Watson's Holmes tales have appeared in dozens of anthologies with various publishers much to the delight of his fans. He is well versed in the original Conan Doyle Canon and his stories are magnificently annotated.

In this new collection aptly called "The Incunabulum of Sherlock Holmes," I.A. Watson delivers six imaginative stories exploring the many facets of the Great Detective and his loyal companion. Each is a rare gem chronicled by a master storyteller. We advise you make yourself comfortable, brew some tea and get ready for a wonderful reading experience as only a Watson can provide. Yes, dear readers, once again, the game is afoot.

THE INCUNABULUM OF SHERLOCK HOLMES

I.A. WATSON

AN AIRSHIP 27 PRODUCTION

PULP FICTION FOR A NEW GENERATION!
AIRSHIP27HANGAR.COM

NEW **PULP**

www.ingramcontent.com/pod-product-compliance
Lightning Source LLC
Chambersburg PA
CBHW051127260626
47170CB00005B/1707